The first odd  s that Annalee r

Not too unusual, unless you knew the dogs were one way she discouraged visitors from getting out of their cars. Then he realized she wasn't holding her trademark shotgun.

He stepped out of his truck and faced the unarmed lady of the mountain. Maybe it would turn out to be a good day after all. "Mornin'," he called.

"Morning, Deputy Ben," she answered, her voice cautious but not unwelcoming.

He walked toward the porch. About ten paces from the steps, the bigger of the two dogs gave a low warning growl.

"Did you ever find that lost girl?" she asked unexpectedly.

There was nothing strange about the question, since he'd been up there two days before, searching for the girl. The strange thing was how she'd raised her voice when she asked it. He was close enough to hear her if she whispered. Her tone made him want to turn around to see if someone was standing behind him.

"No, we haven't found her. But we have some information on her. Name's Theresa Smith. Seems there's a bench warrant for her arrest. She's a witness in her boyfriend's drug possession trial. There are a lot of people who want to talk to her."

Dear Reader,

When I look over my books, I realize that I write about families. Sometimes that's difficult to see because I don't present the usual, mom-dad-and-the-kids families. The families in my stories are made up of disparate parts—broken pieces of love and leftover hope.

In this story, I bring you Annalee, a heroine who is as far from normal as most people can imagine. Yet, she's strong and caring and willing to fight for those she loves. She's not shy about using a shotgun to do it, either. She is also a woman who is worthy of love even though she doesn't believe it.

And what kind of hero can stand up to a woman with a gun? Why, a policeman, of course. Deputy Ben Ravenswood is the kind of man who is slow to judge and quick to offer help when trouble strikes. He's a strong shoulder to lean on and a steady heart to depend on. He knows Annalee deserves love and a future; all he has to do is keep her from running away so he can convince her.

I hope you enjoy *Annalee and the Lawman*.

Best wishes,

Lyn Ellis

P.S. Write to me at P.O. Box 441, Bowie, MD 20718

Annalee and the Lawman
Lyn Ellis

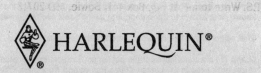

HARLEQUIN®

TORONTO • NEW YORK • LONDON
AMSTERDAM • PARIS • SYDNEY • HAMBURG
STOCKHOLM • ATHENS • TOKYO • MILAN • MADRID
PRAGUE • WARSAW • BUDAPEST • AUCKLAND

ISBN 0-373-70963-3

ANNALEE AND THE LAWMAN

Copyright © 2000 by Virginia Ellis.

To Nance, my "little" sister:
Don't forget to let your star shine.

To my mom, Amelia, just because…

CHAPTER ONE

THE TIRES ON DEPUTY Benjamin Thomas Ravenswood's patrol car spun once before digging into the gravel of the steep winding road leading to the top of Rain Mountain. The unpaved and poorly maintained access was enough to keep most casual traffic to a minimum. The well-maintained No Trespassing signs punctuated with Violators Will Be Shot, were enough to effectively scare off the rest.

The higher he went, the more ominous the warnings became until at last, near the top, he knew he was close to his destination. The sign simply read Turn Around NOW, and a dead crow hung from one of the wooden fence posts.

The Crazy Woman of Rain Mountain.

Ben slowed to a stop and looked to his right down the overgrown road crowded with blackberry canes and wild rose bushes, the road that led to her cabin. You couldn't get down that road without more than a few scratches, either on your car or on your skin. But he couldn't turn around, as the sign suggested.

For the past few months, he'd made it his mission to find a way to reach Annalee Evans. Each time he'd seen her in town, striding along the street with her two intimidating dogs, he'd made an effort to engage her in conversation. He'd tried the weather, local politics, even Braves baseball. So far, she'd kept him at a distance as she did everyone in Dalton Falls. Well, today he had to speak to her, whether she wanted to or not.

Ben shook his head and shifted his car into low to navigate the steep turn. He wasn't truly worried. He could charm nearly anybody, speaking Southern-ese with his aw-shucks, down-home accent. Anna wouldn't shoot him, not right off the bat anyway. And, if he'd miscalculated and she did shoot him, well, he could think of worse ways to go. A charge of assault with a deadly weapon would certainly enhance Annalee's reputation, the one she seemed so happy to hide behind. The headline would read Wayne County Sheriff's Deputy Ben Ravenswood Shot By—depending on who wrote it—Angel/Amazon/Witch/Crazy Woman Of Rain Mountain.

Getting close to Annalee might be worth it. Annalee Evans, in his opinion was one of the most interesting and puzzling people in the county. It didn't hurt that she was beautiful, as well, no matter that she did her best to hide it by keeping her long hair pulled back under a cap and wearing serviceable but loose-fitting clothes. She worked at being unremarkable without much success. Ben had always been good at figuring out someone's story—at least enough to categorize the person. But there was no category for Annalee beyond definitely odd, unpredictable and, by anyone's measure, dangerous.

Ready, or not. Here I come.

THE STRIDENT BARKING of her dogs, Diva and Hunter, brought Annalee Evans from her office to her front window. She carried the loaded shotgun she always kept propped in a corner by the front door. Annalee needed to know she could put her hand on that gun anytime, whether in the rosy light of dawn or the pitch-black dark of a moonless midnight. The shotgun was her equalizer, her guarantee that no one would trespass into her life ever again. Uninvited visitors who weren't discouraged by two ninety-pound-plus Doberman pinschers would most likely reconsider their options in the face of a double-barreled welcome from the lady of the mountain.

Annalee Evans wanted to be alone. As a matter of fact, she insisted on it.

The dogs backed down the gravel driveway, barking and circling while the car rolled to a stop. Annalee unlatched the heavy, reinforced front door, opened it and walked out onto the porch, the shotgun cradled in her arms. The dogs immediately returned to stand at the foot of the stairs, their barks changing from warning to interest. Whether they recognized the occupant of the county police car was doubtful, although by the change in their greeting, they would give the visitor half a chance. Unless Annalee told them otherwise.

Slowly the driver's-side door of the car opened and a man stepped out. The dogs had gone completely silent. With calm and deliberate moves, the officer settled his hat on his head then leaned his forearms on the top of the car door, keeping his hands in plain sight.

Anna recognized Deputy Ben.

He nodded toward her. "Miz Annalee." One hand eased toward Hunter, the bigger of the two dogs. "It's a wonder those dogs haven't killed somebody. What do you need such mean animals for? You doin' something illegal up here?"

Annalee looked proudly at Hunter, her big baby boy who could lie at her feet and whine for attention, or tear off a man's arm if she ordered it. Then she looked back toward Deputy Ravenswood, the closest thing she had to a friend in Wayne County. Well, not friend exactly. She had no friends and intended to keep it that way. But Deputy Ben might be called an ally. He was the only citizen of Dalton Falls, the closest town, who didn't seem to judge her by gossip. The only man who would have the balls to joke about her dogs. The one man who made her pulse rate jump and her insides jittery each time she saw him, or heard his voice.

"Don't you know?" she said in her best fake British accent—one she was sure a witch would use. "I've been setting traps in the woods for children. I bake 'em in the oven then the dogs and I chow down."

"Now I know why they look at me that way," he answered with a slow grin. "They figure if the small ones are good, the bigger ones must be better."

Deputy Ben had a point about being bigger. If his tall, solidly built frame was measured as a meal, he'd be breakfast, lunch and dinner for at least a year. The resulting mental image of nibbling on Deputy Ben was rather unsettling. Of all the men she'd been required to deal with in the past fifteen years, for some reason Ben Ravenswood was the only one who could get to her. From the age of fourteen, it had been her policy that any man who tried to talk to her, or looked at her for too long, was the enemy and had to be warned off. She wouldn't be caught by surprise again—ever. But from the first time she'd run into Ben on one of her infrequent visits to town and he'd done his best to make small talk about the weather, something about him made her want to reach out rather than pull away.

She had no idea why, at this time in her life, such an impulse would occur. She'd given up feeling a very long time ago and reinvented her life along the careful, logical lines she could handle. *Change your name, change your hair, change your home. Run away, run away, hide.*

Anna certainly never intended to let Ben know her weakness for him. Admitting it to herself had been dangerous enough. Each time he looked at her, she had to remember to keep her distance, not to smile or encourage casual conversation. She couldn't relax. She had nothing to offer, and there was nothing she could take from Ben. Best to remember that.

Ready to get back to the point, Annalee shifted the shotgun in her arms, positioning it more in his direction but down, toward the ground. This was the first time he'd driven up the mountain and she needed to know why. Maybe she'd been wrong about him, maybe he was trouble after all. She needed to know one way or the other. He hadn't come up one of the worst roads in the county to discuss the weather or her dogs. "What exactly brings you up here? None of the town's children have gone missing in a while," she said.

And I didn't ask for a courtesy visit.

"Well...actually, we do have a missing person. A teenage girl was involved in an auto accident over on the interstate. She made it into the woods but we can't find her. Even the dogs have lost the trail." He gave Hunter a dark look as if all dogs were wayward.

"That's over five miles from here. She can't have gotten this far. I haven't seen her."

"I didn't figure you had," the deputy said, his Southern accent growing more pronounced. "We're just doin' a grid search and none of the other boys will come up this side of the mountain. The dogs will only go if we boot 'em. I got elected to notify you. You have some kind of spell on this valley?"

If only she did. Maybe then she'd finally feel safe.

"Could be a spell," she answered, playing into her role of the Witch of Rain Mountain. "Or could be just good sturdy barbed wire and—" she nodded toward the dogs "—my caretakers here. Then of course there's my reputation." Annalee raised the shotgun for the full effect.

Both the deputy's hands came up. "I get the picture," he said, and started to get back in the car.

"Good luck with your search," Annalee called. "Just don't search around here."

As BEN BACKED HIS CRUISER up the steep gravel driveway to the turnaround, he growled to himself not unlike one of the unfriendly dogs who'd greeted him. Annalee could be just plain exasperating. Holed up here on her private mountain like some kind of new millennium survivalist. Didn't anyone ever teach her that most normal folks didn't live in complete seclusion? The ones who had the keys to the front door, anyway.

He didn't buy the story that she was crazy. He'd seen crazy during his years as a police officer, and she wasn't that. Nope, she spoke well enough, although her accent wasn't Southern, and she seemed to have no trouble taking care of herself without obvious employment. Her clothes were casual but expensive. Someone like Anna would have an Eddie Bauer catalog. Her boots alone probably cost two hundred dollars.

Not to mention those dogs. You didn't pick up pedigreed and police-trained dogs at the local pound.

What did someone do to drive you up here on this mountain, Annalee?

Cops were paid to be nosy, and Ben had enough time on his hands to be nosier than most. He'd never really adjusted from the nonstop workload of an Atlanta police officer to the slow-paced community service of a Wayne County sheriff's deputy. After turning the patrol car around, he glanced in the rearview mirror and shook his head. The dogs were following him to the end of the driveway, just in case he didn't keep his distance. They were as suspicious as their owner.

Ben knew Annalee would tell him her business wasn't any of his. And she'd be within her rights as long as she didn't use that shotgun to shoot anyone. He felt sorry for the girl they were searching for if she, by some stroke of bad luck, ended up on Rain Mountain. If the dogs didn't eat her alive, the owner surely would.

Twenty minutes later, as he pulled onto the main dirt road at the foot of the mountain, one of the other deputies flagged him down.

"Well, I don't see any major holes in you," Wally Dean said with a chuckle.

"Yeah? Keep laughing and next time you'll have to go up there," Ben said, but he didn't mean it. Ben respected Wally as a deputy, but he'd never let him try to deal with Annalee. The man had the negotiating skills of a billy goat.

"Shoot," Wally said before spitting on the ground. "I'd take every man on the shift with me. My wife told me some of the things people say have gone on up there."

Ben shook his head but asked the question anyway. "And what things have gone on according to JoLynne?"

Wally glanced up toward the mountaintop as if the occupant might, by some supernatural sense, be able to hear him. "You know, spooky stuff, like that woman shooting anything that moves then hanging the dead animals in the trees. She don't even eat 'em, can you imagine?''

Ben could very well imagine it if he believed any of those stories to begin with. Yes, he'd seen a dead crow, but many small farmers hung dead crows from poles in their cornfields. The original scarecrow. He'd have to see more evidence if he—

Wally leaned closer and grinned. "Hell, I even heard she walks in the woods under the full moon, naked as a newborn. What d'ya think of that?''

Unable to stop it, Ben's mind formed a vision of Annalee tall and pale walking in the trees with her long dark hair swinging free. He felt several parts of his anatomy warm to the thought. The idea of Wally ever trying to investigate Annalee soured the growing heat. They'd call her a witch or crazy. If Ben found her that way, he would probably shuck his clothes and follow her into the woods. He'd guard her as closely as those two dogs and keep her safe from whatever had scared her into choosing a twelve-gauge as her only friend.

Maybe she was a witch after all if she could affect him so deeply. Like the old sailors lured onto the rocks, Annalee called to him in a voice only he could hear.

Maybe he was the one going crazy.

Sorry he'd asked Wally in the first place, Ben decided to get back to police business. ''I think if we leave her alone, she'll leave us alone. She said she hasn't seen anyone up there. And believe me, those dogs would never miss a girl struggling through the woods.''

''It's a puzzlement why that girl took off. If she'd stayed on the interstate she would have gotten help a lot quicker. She must've hit her head or something.''

Privately Ben was beginning to think there was more to the teenager's disappearance than either the county police or the girl's mother, who'd been contacted, knew. The girl's boyfriend was ominously uncommunicative on the matter. He kept repeating the story that she got scared after the accident and ran for help. The other two teenagers in the car backed him up. Ben had wanted to ask the young man why she'd run up a mountain rather than down to the next exit, but it hadn't been his interrogation. He'd been called in off duty to help with the search.

''Now that you're safe and sound, I guess we ought to head over to the group on Route 214,'' Wally said, spitting again. ''I still think we're looking too far away for her. Hell, if she made it across three mountains since day before yesterday then we ought to give her an Olympic gold medal.''

Ben nodded his agreement then shifted in the seat to glance up Rain Mountain again. A feeling of foreboding ran through him. He'd had those before. Most cops called it gut instinct. Ben called it "too little, too late." Usually when he had that feeling, something was already underway. Something he rarely could stop. He stared hard at the stand of pines and oaks near the ridge where he knew Annalee Evans's cabin was hidden.

Don't shoot her, Annalee. She's just a kid.

TRANSCRIPTION of taped session with female minor X, 14 years old. Excerpted from psychiatric evaluation of Dr. Antony Desillio, Ph.D., State of New York.

"The man said he didn't mean to."

"But he did."

"I had to do what he said anyway. Because I belonged to him. That's what he said. And no one was coming to help me.

(Pause)

"No one did. I kept waiting but nobody came. Nobody helped me."

"You know that everyone wanted to help you? Don't you?"

"They couldn't find me. The bad man said they'd never find me."

"But they did find you later, didn't they?"

(Long pause in tape)

"No. I found them."

CHAPTER TWO

AS ANNALEE SAT ON her front porch and watched the last rays of the late summer sun filter through the trees, the familiar edginess settled over her. There was no concrete reason for her to be afraid of the dark. After all, years ago she'd been snatched in the middle of the afternoon out of a public parking lot. Kidnapping did not require darkness. Alone and terrified, she'd had to wait through that terrible day until dark to find out what would happen to her.

She had more reason to be afraid of the moon.

Her current unease, however, wasn't the childish nightmare of known or unknown bad men. It was the nerve-jangling approach of change. Something was different. She could feel it in the rustle of the trees, the hushed movements of the small things in the woods. Even though she'd remained hidden and uncooperative in her self-imposed exile, the world around her seemed to have shifted.

Trouble.

Annalee crossed her booted feet and dropped one hand onto Hunter's warm head. After Deputy

Ben left, she and the dogs had walked the acreage surrounding the cabin, checking the spirit chasers and traps she'd built with grim satisfaction. Annalee's spirit chasers weren't the benign carvings and weavings filling the shops in tourist towns. She'd made hers with her own hands and with every ounce of determination she'd developed over the past fifteen years. Meant to intimidate, some were woven from rope, others crudely carved, each included at least one skeletal or mummified animal. All of them were macabre enough to give any uninvited visitors shivers down their spines, and to turn them back before they reached the traps.

The traps weren't for animals, they were for people. She wanted anyone tramping through these woods to know they didn't belong here, and falling into a hidden hole deep enough to sprain an ankle was better than the alternative. The spirit chasers and traps were the second warning, since an intruder would have to cross a sturdy fence and pass a No Trespassing sign to get caught up in them. The final warning would come from Annalee's shotgun.

The idea of a teenage girl on her own wandering around in the woods nagged at Anna. Once she'd been lost and alone and running. She remembered hiding in the dark...trying to sink into the shadows and disappear. Men were searching the mountains for this girl. They would find her. Only the bad man had been searching for Annalee.

She gazed up at the bright sky. The weather would be clear, that should help.

Annalee shook her head to drive away the tight, fear-choked feeling. Why was she worried? The girl wouldn't get this far. She'd find a road to follow or a house with a Good Samaritan. Lost in the possibilities, Anna realized with a start that the sun had dipped below the facing mountain and full dark would be coming on fast now. She needed to go inside, yet she remained on the porch watching the gathering gloom.

"She'll be all right, Hunter," she said as her fingers slid over the big dog's brow. "No need for us to be out looking for her." Hunter moved closer and rested his heavy head on her knee. But Anna felt a tremor move through him as though every nerve under his fur was ready for a fight, or a hunt. He felt it, too.

Trouble.

Pushing away the feeling of impending doom before it accompanied her to bed and danced into her dreams, Anna rose from her chair and, followed by her dogs, went inside. She had paperwork she'd neglected, and dinner to cook. But before she did anything else, she checked her shotgun, then she locked the door.

BEN RAVENSWOOD WAS HAVING trouble sleeping. As far as he could see, the A's and the B's of this case didn't get you to C. None of it made any sense. Not a girl, alone, running off into the woods. Not a woman, full grown, determined to hole up on a mountain. He punched the pillows behind his head and stared out his window at the night sky. A waxing moon was rising and his imagination traveled back to Wally's story of Annalee walking naked under the full moon.

In his parents' house, which he'd inherited when they died, a good fifteen miles away from Rain Mountain, Ben pushed up on one elbow for a clear view of the moon. No, not full yet. But the moon's insufficiency didn't stop his memory from painting a silvered picture in his mind.

He'd been out camping a few years before and once again hadn't been able to sleep. There'd been a high full moon that night and he'd hiked down to the edge of the Cohutta River to watch the water splash and sparkle. As he'd sat, still and quiet, two deer had come out of the trees—one with an eight-point rack worth any hunter's best try, the other a doe, her white tail twitching nervously. The moon had tipped the stag's horns with silver and his proud head with white as he waited for the doe. They cautiously began to drink from the sparkling water, and it was the most beautiful thing Ben had ever been privileged enough to witness.

So the image of Annalee, her skin dusted by moonlight, moving through the trees like a graceful doe had true meaning for Ben. An enlightening effect on his mind, an enlarging effect on another part of his anatomy. A pretty sad testimony to his love life.

Love.

He'd been in love once. And he'd had enough college-level psychology to recognize that he'd never come to grips with Sharon's death. Hell, it had taken everything inside him to get through the official investigation and to face her family. He had to give them credit for not coming right out and saying he'd killed her. Even though that's what had happened.

The police counselor had patiently explained the long process of guilt and grief, but back then Ben hadn't been listening. His mind was stuck, obsessively going over every detail, every action of that night. Cataloging every decision he'd made that had ended in Sharon's death. He had to understand what had gone wrong. Then he'd be able to grieve.

Five years had passed since his well-organized life had had several pages ripped from the calendar. He was no closer to the why of it, but he had let it go. Put it away. As much as he ever would, anyhow.

He had life, which was more than Sharon had been given. He'd live it the best he could, but love, love was a different story. He felt as though his insides had been frozen too long to ever see a spring thaw. One of his buddies on the Atlanta force had told him his heart was as hard as his head. He was inclined to agree.

But he could still help people, still protect and defend. He was good at that—except when it had come to protecting his own.

Ben rubbed his eyes with the heels of his hands and frowned. He guessed he wasn't gonna be able to let this "mystery of Annalee" go on any longer. Not because half the county wanted to know more about her, but because Ben Ravenswood had to know the truth. Maybe then he wouldn't worry about her, or think about her, or wonder whether she practiced witchcraft and howled at the moon. He'd know.

He didn't think she'd tell him, though. It wouldn't be that easy. Just like finding the missing teenager should have been easy and wasn't. He was going to have to take things into his own hands, Ben decided. The best way to search for the girl and to watch Annalee would be from the woods on Rain Mountain.

Ben Ravenswood decided he needed to go camping for a few days. Ten minutes later he was sound asleep.

BY DUSK THE NEXT EVENING Annalee had nearly put her earlier apprehension behind her when something set off the dogs. Barking and growling, Hunter and Diva headed to the windows on the west side of the cabin, away from the road. Annalee ordered them to silence and waited. It could be hunters on the ridge, or a black bear rambling through, no need to panic.

The dogs remained on guard, however, never taking their wary gazes from the trees. With a sigh, Annalee went to put on her hiking boots and get her gun. She knew she wouldn't be able to relax until she was sure that whatever or whoever had bothered the dogs had moved out of range of the house. And she needed to be quick. It was getting dark.

On the way up the first hill, the woods seemed extraordinarily quiet to Annalee. It was early September, moving into fall, and the trees should have been noisy with migrating birds. She strained her ears to hear anything beyond her own footsteps and those of the dogs in the leaves littering the ground. She heard nothing.

At the top of the rise, Diva and Hunter became even more agitated and whined to be allowed to run, but Annalee waited. She had her gun, her equalizer, but she didn't like letting the dogs get too far ahead of her. More for their protection than her own. A bear might attack, or a poacher might shoot rather than face them.

Unable to hold in his exuberance, Hunter barked

several times then guiltily glanced at Annalee. They'd been schooled by the best trainers in the country, but they were still dogs. They wanted to do what dogs do.

"All right, go!" she ordered with a wave of her hand. The dogs raced away like two daredevils shot from a cannon.

Setting off after them as fast as she could, Annalee kept track of them by the loud crashing of the underbrush in their wake. Making her own way through the gradually thickening branches and laurel bushes, Annalee received a sizable scratch on her left hand and swore to put them on leash next time so they couldn't disappear so quickly.

Then, suddenly, the dogs began barking and growling as if they'd caught something and decided to tear it apart. They wouldn't do it, but whatever they'd cornered didn't know that.

A bear, Annalee thought as she pushed herself to move quickly up another hill. They wouldn't put up such a racket over a rabbit or raccoon. She was too far away to see anything. And with her own breath rushing in her ears from the exertion of running in boots, it was difficult to sort out the different animal growls and sounds. But then, piercing through the clear mountain air, she heard a woman scream.

Annalee stopped dead, put down her gun and tried to catch her breath to whistle. The first time she put her fingers in her mouth, she didn't have enough spit to make more than a wheeze. Finally, on the third try, she let out a shrill sound that wouldn't mean anything to anyone except her dogs.

The barking stopped.

Picking up her shotgun, Annalee glanced up at the sky. She could see the first stars winking through the trees. Twilight. The moon wouldn't rise for a few hours and, luckily, it wouldn't be full. She felt in her pocket for her flashlight but decided not to use it yet. Better to see what the dogs had gotten her into first.

Diva whined as Annalee pushed her way through the underbrush. Both the dogs immediately moved to her side but kept their eyes on the huge oak they'd been guarding. Anna could see that someone was crouched inside the rotted-out base of the tree. She steadied her shotgun over one arm then reached into her pocket with her other hand and switched on the flashlight.

The girl started at the light but not enough to scream again. From the terrified look on her face, the dogs had scared her into silence. Annalee lowered the gun but didn't approach her.

"Are you hurt?" she asked. She knew the dogs wouldn't bite without an order, but the girl might have hurt herself trying to get away.

The teenager hugged her knees a little tighter

until her knuckles whitened. She shook her head no.

"Are you the girl everyone's searching for?"

She gazed up toward the light and, for a moment, she looked as if she might say yes. But something stopped her.

"Do you want me to call someone? The police?" Annalee thought of Deputy Ben. If she'd been running and hiding, dirty and alone, she'd want someone to call a man like him. Something in his manner indicated all help, no force. "I know a deputy I can call—"

"No," the girl said, her voice trembling. "I don't want—I can't go back." The last few words were stronger, defiant.

Diva whined again and shifted on her feet. The girl's attention zeroed in on the dogs once more and she swallowed visibly.

"How old are you?"

"I turned eighteen the tenth of last month," the girl answered.

Annalee had to believe she was telling the truth. Liars rarely gave the exact day of their birth. But the girl didn't look eighteen at the moment. Fear could do that, though. Fear could make even someone who thinks she's grown into a child again.

"Do you know you're on private property?" Annalee tilted her hear toward the east. "My cabin is back over that way."

The girl simply stared at her.

"Do you know where you're headed?"

After a long hesitation, the girl nodded.

For the first time Annalee wished she had a closer neighbor. She could send the girl in that direction then call the authorities. As it was, she didn't feel right about marching the girl to the cabin at gunpoint and turning her in. Especially if she had good reason to run. Who was Annalee to pass judgment or force someone to do the "right" thing? Doing the right thing hadn't helped her. She had to let the girl make her own decisions just as she herself had had to do.

"Stand up so I can see for myself that you're not hurt," Annalee ordered. When the girl made no movement, Anna shifted the gun in her arms. Responding to the implied threat, the girl slowly pushed up out of her hiding place.

She was taller than Annalee had expected but on the thin side, with tangled blond hair streaming over her shoulders. Her clothes—jeans and a baggy shirt—were torn and dirty, and there were several reddened scratches on her arms, but she'd managed to hold on to the battered leather purse over her shoulder. She was also obviously pregnant.

Damn. It took a few moments for Annalee to recognize the implications. This pregnant girl had scrambled through the woods for miles and eluded police along with whoever else might be chasing her. A shimmer of admiration ran through Anna.

"You've got to be hungry."

"I could eat one of those dogs, if they didn't eat me first," the girl responded. It sounded like a joke, but she didn't smile and her legs were trembling.

"Follow me to the cabin—"

"I can't go back, ma'am." A statement, no elaboration.

Annalee was about to lose patience. It was only divine justice she supposed, to put someone in her path even more uncommunicative than herself.

"Well, you can't stay here. If you want to feed that baby then come to the cabin. I'll leave some food and a blanket on the porch."

The girl looked at the dogs.

"I'll put the dogs up, until moonrise. If you don't take the food by then you'd better have moved on. I'm going to call the law first thing in the morning."

The girl nodded in understanding.

Annalee didn't like the deal but knew no other way. If she could at least get some food into her, then she wouldn't feel bad about calling Deputy Ben in the morning. There was no way the girl could make it too far at night in these unfamiliar woods.

The dogs kept glancing back as Annalee steadily

led the way to her home. It was the first time she'd ever invited anyone there, and the fact that the invitation had been turned down seemed fitting. She'd done her best to scare everyone away. This girl was an outsider, someone who didn't have the sense to be afraid of the Crazy Woman of Rain Mountain. Or she was someone who had other, larger things to fear.

When they crossed the last rise and the cabin came into view, the girl stayed in the trees as Annalee strode to her own front door.

With efficient hands, Annalee finished the dinner she'd begun cooking earlier. Thirty minutes later, she switched on the porch light then cautiously glanced out the door before taking out a tray with baked chicken, green beans and a baked potato. She'd also put two apples, some cheese and several slices of bread in a paper sack. Dinner for here and breakfast to go. The final additions were a large glass of milk and a bottle of water.

That ought to hold you until I can get Deputy Ben up here, Annalee thought. She dusted her hands and stared into the darkness. Now come and get it before some fat raccoon finds it first.

"The dogs are inside!" she called to the surrounding trees, then turned to go back inside herself. She didn't like the feeling of being in plain view without her shotgun. There was always the possibility the girl wasn't as alone as she appeared.

After reentering her sanctuary, Anna locked the door, turned out the porch light and tried to ignore the welcome, yet unwelcome, stranger in the woods.

BEN HAD HAD TO POSTPONE his camping expedition for twenty-four hours. He'd been called to an area to the east of town where a large part of the search was being conducted. It seemed that a surveyor thought he'd spotted two people in the woods.

Most of the county deputies and several volunteers had spent the day combing the area but found nothing. By the time he'd gotten back to Dalton Falls, it had been too late to hike into a campsite and set up a base. He, along with the other authorities, was beginning to worry they might find a body rather than a lost girl.

He was just pulling into the Sheriff's Department lot when a call came over his police radio. "Be advised—the subject, one Theresa Smith, is wanted on a Fulton County bench warrant to appear as a material witness in a drug trial. Boyfriend, James Cintero, arrested on aggravated assault and drug possession."

"Bingo," Ben said under his breath. No wonder they couldn't find her. She either didn't want to be found, or someone else had found her first.

Ben waved to the deputy at the desk as he en-

tered the duty room. Without slowing down, he
went into the office to use the phone. He had a
couple of old friends in Atlanta. They could find
out more about Theresa Smith. While he was at it,
he decided to put out a few inquiries about Annalee
Evans. Forewarned is forearmed, he decided, because sooner or later he had the feeling he was
going to have to deal with them both.

TRANSCRIPTION of taped session with female minor X, 14 years old. Excerpted from psychiatric
evaluation of Dr. Antony Desillio, Ph.D., State of
New York.

*"He said he liked to touch me and I had to let
him."*

"Where did he touch you?"

*"All over. But especially my hair. He said I had
the prettiest hair, prettier than his other little girl."*

"Did you ever see this other girl?"

"No. He said she died before I came."

"Did he hurt you?"

*"Sometimes he…yes, it hurt. But he taught me
to be still like a stone statue. If I didn't stay still
he would get the tape."*

"Tape?"

*"On my hands, and my feet…on…m-my…
m-mouth."*

(Several gasping breaths)

"It's all right, you're safe now."

*"I can't breathe! No. No. Never safe! No tape.
It makes me sick! It makes me..."*

(More gasping. Sound of intercom buzzer)

CHAPTER THREE

RUN AWAY, RUN AWAY. HIDE.

Annalee awoke to the squawking of crows. She'd been dreaming of running, of hiding from…him. The man who'd hurt her, who'd stolen her faith in ''happily ever after.'' She released the breath she'd been holding. Better that dream than the others.

Glad to see the dim, pinkish light of dawn illuminating the front windows, she stretched. The action caused a book to fall from her chest to the rug-covered floor with a thump. Giving in to a huge yawn, she realized that she must have fallen asleep on the couch. But she hadn't meant to, she'd meant to—a sharp jolt of alarm ran through her.

The dogs.

She'd let them out for their run after moonrise and then settled down to wait for them to come back. Anna pushed to her feet, crossed the room and unbolted the front door.

The porch was empty. No Diva, no Hunter.

Annalee whistled, loud and long. Only the eerie

silence of the trees answered her. No wind, no loping footsteps.

Quickly Anna went back inside to pull on her boots. Then she grabbed her shotgun and hurried down the front steps. If anything had happened to her dogs she'd have no compunction about using the shotgun on the culprit who'd hurt them—animal or human. Diva and Hunter were the only warm-blooded creatures she knew she could trust, and that included the entire human race. Deputy Ben's image interrupted her tally of the many people who had hurt her, either by trying—and failing—to help or by selling her out for money. Maybe she could trust Deputy Ben.

But unlike any other human, her dogs depended on her.

With her heart pounding in her chest, Annalee took deep breaths of the cool morning air to clear her head and to calm her fear. How could she have fallen asleep leaving Diva and Hunter outside? Without them she'd be totally alone.

Although a heavy dew had fallen, Annalee could see no evidence of any disturbance as she circled the house. Suddenly a movement at the edge of the trees caught her attention. A doe stood motionless there. Her ears twitched once, then before Annalee could draw in a startled breath, the doe gracefully leaped uphill, disappearing into the trees.

Not a good sign. If a deer felt safe enough to

get this close to the cabin, the dogs must be far from the area. So, without further clues, she set off up the hill they usually traveled to do their fence check. The dogs might have gone that way out of habit. They wouldn't have run away, but they could have been lured. Her hands tightened on the shotgun as she ducked under the lower branches of a white pine.

Every twenty or thirty feet, Anna would stop to listen. The arching trees overhead caused sound to carry for long distances. The birds had begun calling again. That could be good or bad. Annalee put her fingers into her mouth and whistled for the second time.

The surrounding woods fell silent once more. Then, as she prepared to whistle again, Anna heard a whine. It sounded like Diva; she was sure of it. But why didn't they come?

Expecting something bad, Annalee headed in the direction of the sound. With muscles primed by adrenaline, she pushed through the underbrush and found her normally obedient and ferocious dogs lying in a small clearing, one on either side of the pregnant teenager who was wrapped in the blanket Annalee had left on the porch for her. They'd obviously been there most of the night. The girl appeared to be asleep but the dogs were awake and on guard.

Approaching, Anna took several deep breaths to

get her heartbeat under control, then gave the dogs the low command to come, which they obeyed. Just as she was preparing to scold them for at least ten different rules they'd broken, the girl opened her eyes. She looked more grateful to see Annalee than not. Even the gun didn't seem to faze her.

"Excuse me," she said and scrambling to her feet, she hurried behind the tree.

Annalee waited for her to relieve herself, all the while giving her guilty-looking dogs the evil eye. "You scared me half to death," she grumbled.

"No, they scared *me* half to death," the girl said, returning from her place out of sight. "I thought they were going to bite me. Every time I tried to move they growled. I was afraid to get up and pee."

Still stung with worry about her dogs, Annalee didn't give the girl any slack. "I thought you had somewhere you wanted to go," she challenged.

The girl straightened her back as if she had something tough to say. But then her shoulders slumped and she told what sounded like the truth. "I was tired." She hugged herself against the chilly air. "Too tired. I just fell asleep. Then they came and I was afraid to go."

Making a decision, Anna picked up the blanket and handed it back to the girl. "Come on. I'll fix us some breakfast. You're not staying out here one more night—even if I have to drive you down the mountain myself.''

''But—''

''Not one more night.'' Whether it was the tone of Annalee's voice or the shotgun, the girl followed without further argument. Anna decided to continue what seemed to be working.

When they reached the cabin, she didn't give the girl a choice. She marched over to a padded rocking chair on the front porch and ordered, ''You. Sit, right here.'' After a brief hesitation, the girl sat, wrapping the blanket around herself. Then Annalee eyed her dogs. The same tone of voice wouldn't be a bad choice for two wandering dogs, either. ''You two, come inside and eat your dinner.''

Thirty minutes later, with the sun high enough to sparkle through the trees, Annalee sat on the porch, drinking coffee as she watched the girl eat like a starved puppy. Her own dogs were stretched out on either side of the rocking chair, having already consumed the supper they'd missed the night before.

Annalee decided that the foreman of the construction crew who'd built her cabin must have been psychic. She'd asked him to find her a sturdy rocking chair for the front porch and he'd shown up with two. When she'd challenged him about it, he'd said, ''Well ma'am, you're bound to have visitors.'' Her reply had been, ''I hope not.'' But she'd kept the extra chair.

The girl slowed down as she realized Annalee was watching her. ''Thank you,'' she mumbled with her mouth full. ''You're a good cook.''

Annalee almost smiled, but it had been too long since she'd wanted to, to remember how. Yes, she could cook. In what seemed like another life, she'd learned from a French chef her father had hired. It had filled the hours when she'd been trapped in her home by the notoriety of her name.

''I suppose when you're half starved, anyone can impress you with eggs and ham.'' She waited until the plate was nearing empty before adding, ''There's more if you want it.''

''I might take another biscuit, please.''

Annalee went back inside, poured herself a second cup of coffee and picked up two biscuits. When she returned to the porch the girl seemed more relaxed than she'd been before. Annalee handed over the biscuits and asked a question.

''Have you got a name?''

The girl's hand stopped in mid-reach. ''It's, uh—I can't say. It'll only cause trouble. It's better if you don't know.''

Trouble. She'd felt it in the air. This girl, however, didn't seem to pose a threat. Anna would have questioned her further about how much trouble she could be, but the noise of branches cracking and gravel crunching on the driveway cut that short. The dogs sprang up and watched the road.

"Somebody's coming." Before Annalee could bring herself to take the girl into her home, the girl with the troublesome name snatched the biscuits out of her hand and headed for the woods. "Don't go far," Annalee called. "You know I can find you."

The girl waved in acknowledgment as she pushed into the underbrush. The dogs whined to follow but Annalee ordered them to stay. She saw the flash of a vehicle through the trees. There was no time to go inside for her shotgun.

BEN RAVENSWOOD NOW KNEW more of the story. All the searching in the world wasn't going to bring Theresa Smith out of these woods if she could help it. Just like Annalee, she was a woman being chased by her own past, her own demons.

Driving his four-by-four up to Rain Mountain was a long shot. He only had his instinct to go on. A scary prospect. He'd acted on instinct before and gotten the woman he'd intended to marry killed. Again, he was trying to prevent something, but in this case he didn't even know what that something was yet. He just knew he had to warn Annalee.

The first odd thing Ben noticed was that Annalee didn't let the dogs go. They remained with her on the porch. Not too unusual, unless you knew the dogs were one way she discouraged visitors from getting out of their cars. A darned impressive one at that.

Then he realized she wasn't holding her trademark shotgun.

He stepped out of his truck and faced the unarmed lady of the mountain. Maybe it would turn out to be a good day after all. "Mornin'" he called.

"Morning, Deputy Ben," she answered, her voice cautious but not unwelcoming. "What brings you up here, and on your off time?" she asked.

She was referring to the fact that he was driving his own truck and not wearing his deputy's uniform. Might as well stick to part of the truth. "I'm doing a little hunting over on the Jessup land, to the west." He closed the door to the truck and walked toward the porch. About ten paces from the steps, the bigger of the two dogs gave a low warning growl.

A not so silent "far enough."

Ben stopped and stared into Annalee's eyes. The color struck him, a light golden brown. The color suited her dark hair. The expression in those eyes wasn't fear, more like determination. He glanced around the porch and saw empty dishes on the planks. "You having breakfast outside today?"

For some reason his innocent question startled her. He could see the little jump in the tense line of her shoulders. He'd only been trying to make conversation.

She shoved her hands into her pockets. "Yes."

Okay, then, he thought. No conversation in that direction. He decided she wasn't going to help him out. Then, unexpectedly, she did.

"Did you ever find the lost girl you were looking for?" she asked.

The change of subject surprised Ben. There was nothing odd about the question itself. It was a perfectly normal one to ask since he'd been up there two days before searching and asking questions. The unusual part was how she'd raised her voice when she asked it. He was close enough to hear her if she whispered. Her tone made him want to turn around to see if someone was standing behind him.

"No, we haven't found her. I came up to let you know we have some new information on her. Her name is Theresa Smith. Seems there's a bench warrant for her arrest. She's a witness in her boyfriend's drug possession trial. There are a lot of people who want to talk to her."

A LOT OF PEOPLE. Annalee knew more than she liked about a lot of people wanting to talk, wanting to ask questions. Nosy people were one of the reasons she didn't invite anyone too close.

Her first reaction when she'd seen the strange

truck moving up the driveway was her usual—caution. But when she'd discovered Deputy Ben driving she'd felt a rush of relief. Not usual at all. She'd waited on the porch along with Diva and Hunter until he'd pulled up and shut down the engine. Anna hadn't let the dogs go in case they ignored the new arrival and made a beeline for the girl waiting in the brush. So Ben had practically walked to her front steps.

The foolishness of being alone in the woods this close to a man without her shotgun handy made Anna's head pound. But she wanted to demonstrate she wasn't afraid of him, to give the girl every chance to see she should come out and go with Deputy Ben. He could find her a safe place to stay. He could look out for her.

Those sentiments surprised Anna more than finding the girl hiding in her woods in the first place. What was it about Deputy Ben that made Anna almost trust him?

"So you're looking to arrest her?" she asked, again loud enough for the girl to hear.

Ben rubbed his chin and smiled a harmless, wouldn't-hurt-a-flea smile. "We like to call it protective custody. She wouldn't go to jail."

Anna crossed her arms and waited another long minute, hoping the girl might give it up. She didn't realize she'd been staring at the trees until Deputy Ben turned and looked over his shoulder.

"You see the Green Man?" he asked.

"The what?" Annalee asked in return, amazed she'd been so obvious.

"The Green Man. You know, the mythical man of the forest—like Sasquatch. If you stare into the trees long enough, they say you'll see his eyes, looking back." Ben's smile reappeared and for a moment Annalee wished she could just enjoy it. But she knew better. No matter how much this man made her want to trust him. She'd trusted before and knew if she relaxed, then her world could be turned upside down again. She couldn't allow that to happen.

"Oh, that Green Man. Yeah. I shot him about a month ago—fed him to the dogs. He should have stayed on the far side of my No Trespassing signs."

Deputy Ben laughed and shook his head. "I take your point." He sighed and gazed up at her, almost willing her to let down her guard.

In that moment she discovered he cared about her, was trying to help somehow. Not as policeman to citizen, but person to person—man to woman. The revelation was such a surprise to her dormant social skills, she almost stepped back in shock. Only the residual warmth of long-forgotten memories kept her from retreat.

"Listen, I—" He reached into his top pocket and pulled out a white card. He stepped forward and extended his hand. Both Diva and Hunter gave warning growls stopping him.

Close enough to touch.

Annalee stared down at the card in his long, blunt fingers the way she might look at a welcome sign in the window of a cozy inn—wanting to go in but knowing she couldn't have rest, or welcome…or help.

"Take it," he said in a coaxing voice he might use on a frightened animal. "If the girl shows up, or you need help, call me. It's a cell phone I carry."

Quickly, so as not to give away the trembling in her hands, Annalee snatched the card from him. She wouldn't look him in the eyes. He was too close, and she might do something stupid like tell him the truth. She already knew he was the kind you couldn't lie to easily. The only way she'd managed was through sarcasm rather than answers.

"Thank you," she mumbled, then stuffed the card into the back pocket of her jeans.

Looking as if he'd made some great headway, Ben voluntarily moved back a few steps. "Like I said, I'll be up on the other side of the mountain. If you see the Green Man again, check before you shoot. It might be me." With a wave, he returned to his truck.

TRANSCRIPTION of taped session with female minor X, 14 years old. Excerpted from psychiatric evaluation of Dr. Antony Desillio, Ph.D., State of New York.

"You do know that your father did his best to help you."

"Nobody helped. Just like the bad man said. He said nobody loved me but him."

"Your father loves you very much."

(Long pause)

"He didn't pay the money."

"The police told him that if he paid the ransom, you would be hurt or killed."

"The police don't know everything. I was hurt. The bad man didn't want the money anyway. He wanted me to stay with him and be his little girl. But every day he told me how my other father wouldn't pay the money, how the police had stopped looking. Nobody wanted me back."

"The police did everything they could do to find you. I'm so sorry they didn't."

"They'll never find him, either. He told me so."

CHAPTER FOUR

"WHY DIDN'T YOU GO with Deputy Ben?" Annalee asked impatiently as she waited for the girl she now knew as Theresa to hand over her filthy clothes. She'd threatened to make the girl stay on the porch with the dogs if she wouldn't take a shower.

The rustling behind the bathroom door stopped momentarily, then Theresa's jeans, shirt and underwear were shoved through the opening. "Why didn't you tell him where to find me?" she challenged.

"Because." Annalee huffed and gathered up the clothes. She wasn't about to discuss her reasons with a pregnant runaway who seemed to have more guts than brains. She didn't know why she'd remained silent when she'd had the perfect opportunity to tell Ben, and that confusion made her more nervous than inviting Theresa into her cabin. She pushed the door shut with her foot. "Use the robe hanging on the back of the door until your clothes are dry."

"You know, 'because' hasn't worked on me

since I was five," Theresa taunted through the door, stopping Annalee in the hall.

"Well, it had better work on you today. Take a shower, because you stink. And wash your hair." When the sound of the shower drowned out any other comments, Annalee let the matter drop. She hadn't had any brothers or sisters, and because of her situation, she'd given up on having any children of her own. So how was she supposed to handle this runaway child-woman?

I don't have to handle her, she reminded herself as she stuffed the ragged jeans and shirt into the washing machine. *All I have to do is get her clean enough to sit in my truck so I can drive her down the mountain.* Then she'd be somebody else's problem and Annalee could reestablish her hardwon peace and her well-defended boundaries.

So far, every time you think you're done with her she shows up again, her conscience mocked her as she measured extra soap for the clothes. After she turned on the machine, she reached into her back pocket and pulled out the card Deputy Ben had given her. If worse came to worst, Anna decided, she'd call him and let the law "handle" Theresa.

Unsettled but resigned to her course, Anna switched on a classical music CD and sat at her desk intending to do some paperwork. She'd been so distracted the past few days that even dealing with bankers and trustees seemed restful in comparison.

She also decided that as soon as this temporary crisis resolved itself she would take up another course of study. She'd already studied and written enough to have a degree in veterinary science, although she'd never attended school. She had the time and intellect to learn anything from books, even if she never used the knowledge in the real world.

Forty minutes later, through music and familiar routines, she'd nearly regained her equilibrium when Theresa walked into the living room. Dressed in a pair of Anna's rag socks and wrapped in a fluffy terry robe, Theresa looked like a different girl. A younger and much more pregnant girl. For some reason the robe accentuated her belly rather than hiding it the way the oversize jeans and shirt had.

Theresa must have noticed the increased awareness in Anna's expression, because she seemed reluctant to completely enter the room. It was as if her dirty clothes had been her armor and now she felt exposed.

"Have a seat on the couch. I'll put your clothes in the dryer," Anna said, hoping to sound businesslike. No use stirring things up any more than they already were. When she returned, Theresa was seated on the couch, awkwardly combing the tangles out of her wet hair. Annalee took her place behind the desk again.

She had the vague, long-ago memory of her own mother combing Annalee's hair and clipping barrettes on each side to keep the strands out of her eyes. But as she watched the truculent teenager she'd allowed into her home struggle, she had no motherly urge to help. Those dim memories of her mother were always overpowered by darker memories of having a man, *that* man running his hands through her hair, telling her how pretty it was, how soft to the touch…smelling her scent…

Annalee caught herself before the memory could proceed. She didn't want to think about the memories that came next, and as a defense had trained her mind to stop and return to the present. *No. No. No. Run away, run away.*

She'd learned at a young age to lose herself in a symphony, a book, an old movie, or playing her mother's cello. Happy endings were for other people. She would concentrate on safe places, on living right now in this sunset or that cool breeze. The future meant less than the past; she had no reason to fear it as long as her barriers were intact, but she also had no reason to hurry it along.

Theresa, however, obviously did have a future she needed to manage right now.

They sat in silence for several minutes before Anna asked, "How far along are you?"

Theresa tugged at a particularly resistant tangle then giving up, lowered her hands to her belly. "I don't know for sure," she answered.

"What did the doctor say?"

"I never went to the doctor," Theresa answered. "Didn't have any money, and nobody else cared one way or the other."

"What about your mother, your boyfriend—"

"I don't want to talk about him." A hard look changed her face and seemed to age her by several years. "Her either. And before you ask why, the answer is, because." With one mutinous glance, Theresa went back to working on her hair.

Annalee wanted to say, *I get the message.* But even that gave away more than she could afford. Better to retreat to silence. Silence had become her world and she'd gotten used to it. Why try to change because a stranger had barged or, more accurately, stumbled into her life? Too much information could not only come back to haunt her, it could mean her life. The less they talked the better.

"CAN YOU HEAR ME CLEARER NOW?" Ben asked, after walking to the top of a small rise in the land around him. He waited, then through the intermittent signal, he heard the sheriff's voice.

"Yeah. Loud and clear. Keep me informed."

"Will do."

Ben slipped the phone into the side pocket of

his hunting vest and went back to his campsite. He still needed to set up the tent and secure his supplies. His plan was to stay on Rain Mountain for three or four days on the pretext of hunting. In the meantime, he could thoroughly search the mountaintop, the only area that had not been searched well, for Theresa Smith. If she didn't turn up alive soon, they would have to assume the worst. Her boyfriend had already been transported to the county jail down in Atlanta to await trial on drug charges. But they would need the girl to testify. She couldn't have just disappeared into thin air.

Ben gazed to the east. In that direction, about a thousand yards from where he stood was Annalee's cabin. He knew she was hiding something. From the moment she'd arrived in Dalton Falls, she'd been hiding something. Now the time had come to find out what. If it had nothing to do with the girl, fine. He'd have to admit that his "too little, too late" intuition had failed him. But he couldn't walk away until he knew.

For the life of him, though, he couldn't understand why Annalee would involve herself in anyone else's business—unless she was forced. She'd made a major deal out of keeping to herself, to the point of being rude and letting everyone believe she was crazy.

Surely a woman who built booby traps and carried a shotgun couldn't be forced to do much of anything. Especially by a teenage girl.

Ben shook his head and stooped to unpack his gear. He'd asked the sheriff to let him know if anyone came through with more information on Theresa Smith's background or Annalee's. He had no right to investigate Annalee since she wasn't under direct suspicion, but he'd done it anyway. Couldn't take it back now. It would require some time to do a thorough computer search. Until then, the only way to find out anything new was to search the woods and watch and wait.

"THAT MUSIC IS REALLY PRETTY," Theresa said, her voice sounding dreamy and faraway. "Even if it doesn't have any words."

Annalee looked up from her book. Theresa was dressed in her own clothes now with her long hair combed and dry. Bundled up in an Indian blanket throw on the couch, she seemed half-asleep and much too young to be almost a mother.

"It's Mozart." Anna forced the familiar coolness into her voice. She couldn't allow Theresa to feel too welcome. Without glancing at the girl, she checked at her watch and discovered it was already two o'clock. "It's past lunchtime, are you hungry?"

Theresa's eyes were drifting shut. "No, not really," she managed. "I think I'll just rest here...a minute..."

Before reaching the end of the sentence, she drifted off. Watching Theresa sink into exhausted sleep made something inside Anna give way. The girl was so tired, lost in a world of strangers and still trying to brazen her way through it. This girl and all her problems confirmed Anna's philosophy. What didn't kill you might make you stronger, but it also robbed you of hope and of peace.

Anna pushed to her feet and motioned to the dogs. She'd walk the fence line and leave Theresa to her rest. The girl would need every ounce of her strength to face whatever awaited her.

THE SHOTGUN FELT HEAVY in her hands, heavier than usual. Perhaps because it symbolized what her life had come to. Cold, hard protection. A weapon calculated to instill fear in anyone she faced. After all, it was pretty difficult to miss with a twelve-gauge, and what you hit wouldn't be pretty. As the man who'd taught her to shoot had said, "You point this and pull the trigger. Whoever is bothering you will go away. I promise."

As she hiked up the first rise with the dogs on her heels, she thought of the teenager back at the cabin. *I promise.* Anna hadn't made any promises to Theresa and vice versa. She had no idea if she could trust the girl or not, but as long as she remained in the cabin, Anna would protect her and her unborn baby. It was the one thing Annalee Evans knew how to do.

She'd climbed to the fence line and turned to hike westward when the dogs took off like two black-and-tan ballistic missiles. It required ten minutes of uphill hiking to catch up with them. By that time they were on guard and facing a stand of pines crowded with a tangle of wild azaleas at least eight feet high. Diva and Hunter were both set and growling at one particular area of the green wall. A brief order from Anna would send them into the bushes. But without a better idea of what waited in the tangled branches and leaves, she hesitated. Unable to see anything herself, she raised the shotgun and chambered a round. The distinctive sound of the pump action reverberated through the air.

Nothing moved.

Then a deep male voice said, "Now, there's a sound I recognize."

The dogs barked and whined to be let go. Anna adjusted the aim of her shotgun in the direction the voice had originated but she still couldn't see his face.

"Remember the Green Man?" Wearing camouflage clothes and a shapeless matching hat, Deputy Ben slowly stepped through the bushes with his hands raised. "It's just me, Annalee." When she didn't respond, he continued, "I told you I might be hunting around here."

Anna wasn't sure what to do. For the second time in one day Deputy Ben seemed determined to butt into her life. To trespass on her land. What she couldn't figure out was why? Had he found out about her past? He didn't seem like the type to stoop to blackmail, but then again, people had rarely surprised her by being upstanding rather than self-centered. Maybe he was like the man who'd hurt her. Fascinated by her weakness and her strength. Everything inside her rejected that thought, but she kept the gun raised.

"You know I'm getting tired of you showing up on my property whenever you feel like it. Even deputies are supposed to abide by No Trespassing signs," she said.

BEN SLOWLY LOWERED his hands but his gaze remained on the gun. Standing on her front porch with that shotgun in her hands, she hadn't seemed very intimidating, not for a man trained to face guns. But out here, alone in the woods with only her dogs for help, she looked deadly serious. If he'd imagined her hands would be shaking at a moment like this, he'd been wrong. Her grip on the shotgun was rock steady, all business.

Time to calm the waters. "I'm sorry to keep bothering you," he said. "But I was following a

deer trail and didn't pay attention to the fence."
He gave her what he hoped was a harmless half
smile.

He had a long few seconds to sweat and watch
her think that statement over. Then, slowly, the
tenseness went out of her arms and she lowered
the gun. Some part of him began to breathe a little
easier. He didn't know if he'd been saved by his
excuse or the Southern charm he'd supposedly inherited from his mother's side of the family. Whatever the case, he hadn't intended to provoke her.
After all, didn't half the town believe she was
crazy? Was he some kind of fool to believe something else and test it with his life? Probably. But
it was his life to risk.

"Sit, stay," she said to the dogs. The growling
stopped. "You told me you were going to hunt. I
don't see a rifle," she said as she braced her gun
against her shoulder. "Were you going to wrestle
the deer down, or talk him to death?"

Ben decided it would be best to continue on the
way he had begun with Annalee—by telling the
truth. Lies didn't seem to be working. He rubbed
the tension from the back of his neck with one
hand and shrugged. "Yeah, well, hunting was only
part of it. The main thing is we still have a missing
girl out here somewhere and if we don't find her
soon, she could die in these woods."

With an abruptness he'd seen at other times in

town, Annalee looked away from him and toward the top of the mountain. A combined defense and dismissal. "Seems that if she'd come through here, she would have seen my signs and the fences and gone a different route."

Ben wanted to agree but he couldn't. He shook his head. "This girl is runnin' like the devil himself is on her trail. I get the feeling your signs wouldn't scare her much."

Annalee looked at him then and one side of her mouth kicked up into what could be considered a smile. It happened so fast Ben was barely able to register the privilege of seeing the Crazy Woman of Rain Mountain smile. "Probably not," she said. Then she went serious. "The dogs and I are checking the fence line. If I see anything, I'll let you know."

She'd already taken two steps uphill with the dogs following when he called to her, "Annalee?"

She stopped and turned. With the sun streaming through the trees at her back, lighting her hair and the edges of her clothes, she seemed unreal, almost a hallucination. The brightness in his eyes made them water and the prickling of goose bumps ran along his arms. A trick of the light made her eyes look like molten gold. No wonder people talked about her, called her a witch.

"Will you let me walk up the mountain with you?" he asked. He figured it was worth a try. The

puzzle of Annalee was calling to him louder than
any inner voice of warning. He wished he could
convince her he had good intentions, although
there remained some confusion on that point. He
wasn't sure what he wanted from her, he just knew
he wanted more than she would willingly offer.

She watched him like a seasoned fighter sizing
up the rookie opponent in the opposite corner before backtracking two steps downward, toward
him. He couldn't see any friendliness in her gaze
now, only cold, businesslike assessment. "I don't
know what you want from me but whatever it is,
you need to know this. If you think these dogs
won't attack, or that this gun is loaded with blanks
you are mistaken. If you think you can invade my
privacy or do anything to hurt me without paying
a price, you are doubly mistaken." Then, as if
she'd read his earlier thoughts, she said, "People
talk about me for good reason, Deputy Ben. I am
dangerous. A smart man would listen to what they
say."

"A really smart man would somehow convince
you to help him find that lost girl so he could sleep
at night knowing she was safe."

Annalee stared at him as if he'd surprised her.
The dogs snuffled around his boots and pant legs
as if they wanted to commit his scent to their Ten
Most Wanted list. Ben held his breath.

"Come on, then," she said. Without taking time

to count his current blessings, he and the dogs followed her footsteps.

BEHIND HER, Ben's footsteps made less noise than her own. The man was probably an excellent hunter, she decided, when he actually hunted that is. Today he was looking for Theresa and not knowing what else to do, Anna had instinctively led him away from the cabin. She wouldn't feel good about giving Theresa away when the girl had gone to sleep trusting Anna to keep her secret. She herself understood the concept of an unpleasant awakening.

Trust. There was little enough of it left in the world. Theresa might be a drug dealer or a thief, or a common liar, but Anna wouldn't betray her trust. She'd have to be provoked first.

That went for the man behind her, as well. She glanced back at him when she reached the fence line higher up the mountain. Her warning to him had been real, but deep in her complicated mix of mind and heart, she still trusted him. Maybe she was getting soft at the ripe old age of twenty-nine. Or maybe it was the sound of his voice when he said he wanted to find Theresa so he could sleep without worry.

He'd provoked her. As she'd watched his mouth curl into a half smile in reaction to her attention, she'd experienced a sudden rush of unexplained warmth under her skin. Why in the world would he cause...understanding dawned. Oh, no. She thought she'd outlived the normal female biology of needing a mate. She'd studied it, waited for it to occur. And when it did, she'd dealt with it like so many other challenges in her life. The option to have a partner in life had been stolen from her before she'd had a chance to experience love or honest desire, so the feelings that came much later had had to be squelched.

Perhaps her feeling of trust was a disguise for longing. A wish that the past could be put to rest for once and for all, so she could be free to be normal, to have a husband, a family.

As Anna glanced back, Diva, who was walking in front of Ben, detoured to the left around a tangled pile of vines. One of Anna's booby traps. The dogs knew them well. Better to warn the man.

"Don't step there," she said, pointing toward the spot.

Without pausing, Ben walked around the trap. "You haven't planted anything explosive or lethal in that hole, have you?" he asked as he reached her.

"If you're asking as a policeman, no," she answered. "Although I did encourage two or three big, fat copperheads to make it their home away from home."

Ben smiled again and scratched his chin. "Is

there anything you are afraid of?'' he asked. '''Cause it certainly isn't snakes, or the town of Dalton Falls, or me.''

Anna gazed into his humor-filled hazel eyes and tried to fight the fear that had long ago frozen her life, her heart. It had been years since any man her own age had actually teased her. Although she recognized it, she didn't know how to respond to teasing. The only thing she could offer in return was the truth. For a brief instant, Anna revealed part of herself to Ben. She allowed him to see into the terror she experienced every day.

"There are bad people in the world," she managed to say. "I know, I've felt their touch. One of them anyway." She forced her gaze away before she saw the pity or more questions. She'd said all that needed to be said about the past. "I prefer snakes," she said, effectively closing the subject. "Come on Hunter, Diva, let's move along."

Forty minutes of hiking without conversation later, they found a ragged piece of cloth caught on the fence wire and Anna felt like kicking herself. They'd stopped to rehang one of her shadow catchers that had fallen to the ground when Ben noticed the cloth.

Anna immediately recognized it as a piece of Theresa's blouse, the one she'd washed only a few hours before. There was little doubt Ben recognized it as a clue, as well.

"Looks like she came this way after all," he said, as he systematically searched the area around the fence.

Making an effort to be unimpressed, Anna countered, "That cloth could belong to anyone. It could have been out here for a year." Her heart was pounding. In many ways lying had become natural to her, for self-preservation. But for some reason, lying to Ben seemed like a personal betrayal rather than justifiable expediency.

"This hasn't been out here a year."

With a sinking feeling, Anna moved over to see what else he'd found. Ben held out a pack of matches and a tube of lipstick.

Theresa must have spilled her purse going over the fence. The shapeless, beat-up bag she'd dragged up the mountain had done its best to give her away.

Damn.

"We had rain on Tuesday," Ben said before striking one of the matches. As the flame flared to life, he added, "These matches haven't been wet."

An urgency to get back to the cabin, to tell Theresa what had happened and give the girl the choice of running farther or surrendering to Deputy Ben clutched at Anna.

The only thing she'd promised Theresa was a ride down the mountain. And, as far as she could determine by the interest on Ben's face as he looked first up the mountain then down, now would be the time for Theresa to move. Otherwise, Anna had the feeling that he'd be knocking on the door of the cabin in very short order.

Anna whistled for the dogs before facing Ben. "Well, glad to see you found what you're looking for. I'm gonna head back home." The words came out too fast. Anna took in a breath and searched for her normal distancing defenses.

He didn't say anything right away, he just watched her.

"I've got things to do," she added, then felt like screaming. Why was she making excuses to this man?

Finally, after an extended silence, he said, "Thanks for your help."

Not wanting to say one more word that might give her away, Anna nodded before setting off toward the cabin. The dogs lagged behind because they were used to traversing a longer distance, but Anna cut straight for home.

Thanks for your help.

She hadn't intended to help. She'd intended to distract him. Now she'd led him straight to Theresa's trail. The girl would have to leave now and maybe it was best. Anna wasn't the kind of comfortable host who made her guests feel at home and Theresa needed more help than she could provide. Like a doctor, and someone who loved her enough to look out for her and her baby.

The source of her dilemma was still asleep when Anna returned to the cabin. The sun was sinking behind the western ridge and the wind had picked up a little, making the swaying pines, the dogs and Anna restless.

Trouble.

Tomorrow night would be a full moon. Annalee didn't have to look at the calendar, she could feel its pull under her skin, itching through her thoughts. She had to get Theresa out of her cabin and off her land before she witnessed something people only whispered about.

The Crazy Woman of Rain Mountain.

TRANSCRIPTION of taped session with female minor X, 15 years old. Excerpted from psychiatric evaluation of Dr. Antony Desillio, Ph.D., State of New York.

"Tell me about the moon."
(Extended silence)
"No."

CHAPTER FIVE

"I'M NOT FEELING VERY GOOD," Theresa said when Anna woke her to eat dinner.

Anna had planned to feed the girl one more time, then get her in the truck and take her down the mountain. But now...

"What's wrong?" she asked.

"My back." Theresa grimaced as she pushed to a sitting position on the couch. "And my stomach is upset."

Anna stared first at Theresa, then at her belly. She knew nothing about pregnancy and birth—not in humans, anyway. Her mother had died when she was seven, no time to even hear the story of how she herself had come into the world.

"Do you think it's the baby?" Anna asked, although she figured Theresa would have said so if that were the case. In all the veterinary books Anna had studied, the animal mothers seemed to know when their time had come.

Theresa stretched into a more comfortable position looking completely stumped. "I don't know."

Anna felt the urgent need to sit down and did so on the coffee table facing the couch. "You've got to let me take you to the hospital," she said. "No arguments." Anna stood out of nervousness and to cut short any debate. "I'll feed you first, some soup if you're up to it, but then we go." Decision made, she turned to leave.

Theresa grabbed Anna's arm before she could walk away. "No. I can't go to the hospital. Why can't I stay here?" Her eyes filled with tears, she looked scared to death. "Please," she pleaded.

The feel of Theresa's hand on her wrist nearly made Anna wrench herself away. Very few people had touched her in the past fifteen years, and none of them had gripped her with the intensity or wiry strength of this girl. Anna felt no fear, only surprise and a communicated need. A good sign, it meant she'd recovered to an almost human level. Several levels up from when she'd been a frightened young girl.

Anna sat back down and rested her hand lightly over Theresa's before coaxing her to let go. "Theresa, I don't know a thing about having babies. You're the first woman I've been in contact with who was pregnant." With tears still running down her cheeks, Theresa listened. "When your time comes you need a doctor. What if things go wrong and something bad happens to the baby? If you were here or out in the woods alone, what would you do? What could I do?"

Theresa sniffed and used a sleeve to blot her tears. When she gazed at Anna again, the hard, hunted expression had rekindled in her eyes.

"The baby will die anyway if I go into town."

Anna felt the familiar tightening of anxiety in her chest. What could be so terrible that this girl would risk her baby? Anna wasn't sure she wanted to know.

"What do you mean?"

The girl blew out an exasperated sigh. "Why do you think I'm in the woods hiding in the first place? Why do you think I ran until I fell down and couldn't get up? I thought, after you took me in...I thought you might help me."

"Help you how?"

She still seemed reluctant to tell the whole story, but then whatever was making her sick must have intensified, because she gave in and confessed.

"You know I'm wanted by the law."

Anna remembered very well what Deputy Ben had said. But she didn't see why a girl as strong as Theresa would be afraid. "You're wanted as a witness. You won't go to jail pregnant. They won't hurt your baby."

"They won't," Theresa said in a hard voice, "but he will."

He. A shiver of foreboding ran through Anna.

"He who?"

"Jimmy, my boyfriend. He's told me a hundred times that he'll kill my baby if I open my mouth against him. And the police are gonna make me testify."

A boyfriend, not a terrifying stranger.

Anna started to say the easy thing, the normal thing…if he's in jail, he can't hurt you. *If.* But she knew too well how one man could focus on a fantasy or a threat and never stop until he'd acted it out. If this Jimmy really wanted Theresa's baby dead, he wouldn't stop until he'd accomplished it. Or until someone stopped him.

Anna propped her elbows on her knees and put her hands over her eyes. "Let me think." But her contentious mind said, *Think of what? She cannot stay here.* Still Annalee was finding it harder and harder to turn her away. Desperate, she considered driving her north, to Greenville or Asheville. Anywhere away from Rain Mountain. But if she dropped her off at a hospital, the officials would still demand identification. Theresa would be caught and brought back and Anna would be ruled an accessory. If there was anything she feared, it was the scrutiny of the police and the press. Then, she had an unexpected inspiration. A long shot, but at least a first step toward resolving the situation.

"There's a woman on the other side of the mountain who's supposed to be a midwife. Her

name is Juney something. I don't remember the
last name. I overheard two women in town talking
about her." Anna had eavesdropped on the conversation of the two strangers because the subject
had interested her. It seemed like she herself
wasn't the only woman in the county who was considered a witch. One of the women had said Juney
merely had to put her hand on a pregnant woman's
belly to tell when the baby would come, what sex
it would be and who the father was.

Theresa perked up slightly, although she still
looked pale. "I'll go if you go with me."

"Of course I'll go with you," Anna said, surprised by the girl's uncertainty. Did she think Anna
would push her out the door, point in the right
direction, and watch the girl walk to the other side
of the mountain?

Maybe so. She remembered she hadn't been especially welcoming to Theresa from the beginning.
She'd threatened at one point to sic the dogs on
her even though she hadn't intended to fulfill the
threat.

"Listen, I've got my own reasons for living up
here alone. It has nothing to do with you," Anna
confessed. "Don't take it personally."

Theresa nodded, accepting the words as truth.
She'd obviously been in other places where the
welcome had been less than warm. "Will you let
me stay here on the couch for one more night?"

Anna knew it took a lot for Theresa to ask. If the girl hadn't been pregnant, her strong will would have marched her to Chattanooga or maybe even all the way to Atlanta. But now she was asking for tolerance, and one night of help.

"No, you can't stay on the couch. I expect you to sleep in a bed like a normal pregnant woman." That was as close to a joke as Anna could make and it was weak. Theresa smiled anyway, as though her entire future depended on, and would be solved with, one more night. "There's a guest room two doors past the bathroom. I'll even put some sheets on the bed."

IT WAS AFTER DARK, and Ben should have started back to his camp an hour ago. But he remained where he'd ended up when he'd followed Theresa's trail. At Annalee's cabin. The girl had come this way, he was sure of it. Whether she could pass by without attracting the dogs' or Annalee's attention was doubtful. He remembered the empty breakfast dishes on Anna's porch and now her strange behavior made sense. Had the girl stayed? Or moved on?

The lights were on inside the cabin, and he thought he'd seen someone besides Annalee moving around. He couldn't be sure, though. The dogs would notice if he got too close and then he'd end up with a few teeth marks in him before he could negotiate.

As he chewed on a piece of beef jerky, he tried to imagine what Annalee had had for dinner. Whatever she'd fixed, the smell of it cooking had invaded his hiding place in the woods and made his mouth water. It was enough to make a less cautious man give himself up as a trespasser. He had no doubt, however, that if he approached Annalee's cabin in the dark, dinner would not be what she'd offer him. He'd have a better chance at negotiating with her dogs for food, or mercy.

A few cicadas had begun to buzz in the dark as Ben glanced upward through the trees checking for moonrise. Once the almost-full moon rose over the trees the light would enable him to make his way back to his camp over unfamiliar ground without using a flashlight. Content to sit and watch, he leaned his shoulders against the sturdy trunk of an oak and waited for the dark to "thin out" as his granddaddy used to say.

He could see why Annalee loved this place on Rain Mountain. Remembering her face as she'd said, "I am dangerous," Ben decided that perhaps love was too strong a word. He didn't consider Annalee the sentimental type. But love or not, she'd chosen well. Her home had been built snugly between two arms of a natural valley on the mountainside with a year-round creek running along the north side. Enough trees had been cleared around the cabin to provide a yard and an open patch of sky. Easy to defend and difficult to find. If you walked thirty yards, the cabin would disappear like a mirage.

A shimmer of memory flared. When he and Sharon had first started dating, she'd coerced him with smiles and promises of a warm-evening-after into taking her to a play at one of the local Atlanta playhouses. The play had been a little too "musical" for him, but one part of it had stuck in his mind. It was about a town that simply appeared in the middle of nowhere every one hundred years.

Brigadoon. This place could be that magical. Ben had the distinct impression Annalee's cabin might fade out of sight, along with her at any moment. It was that sense of impending loss that kept him preoccupied with Rain Mountain and its infamous resident. Maybe he'd made some kind of weird connection between the loss of Sharon and the strange situation with the runaway girl. He shook his head as he chewed. No. He knew that couldn't be true, because he'd already had a case for Annalee before the girl showed up or—more exactly—hadn't shown up where she was supposed to be. Maybe the three of them were lost and just didn't know it yet.

Shrugging off dark outcomes, he squinted toward the windows and wished he'd brought his binoculars. They were long-range, for open ground, not worth a damn for searching in the woods. But they were just the ticket for looking into windows and keeping a safe distance. He wanted to see how Annalee spent her time, how she survived on a mountain alone without a neighbor for ten miles. How she didn't need anyone but those dogs and that gun.

He was startled when the front door of the cabin opened, and braced himself for the usual rush of barking and growling.

In front of his eyes, Anna walked out with another woman, helping her down the stairs as though the woman was old or sick. Annalee's truck was parked at the edge of the circle of brightness provided by the porch light so he couldn't make out much more. But as Annalee opened the door to her truck and the interior light came on, Ben realized the woman she helped into the passenger seat was pregnant.

"And who, in the name of Missus O'Grady, is that?" Ben asked like a curse in the dark.

He watched them drive away, then cursed for real that he'd left his truck so far up the mountain. As it was, he jogged up the gravel behind them as fast as he could. Standing at the top of the driveway watching the truck's taillights disappear down the road, he rubbed the back of his neck in frustration.

What did Annalee's odd behavior and protective nature have to do with this pregnant woman no one in Dalton Falls had ever seen? That he'd never seen?

And where was the missing girl?

Ben walked back down the driveway to Annalee's cabin one more time, determined to knock on the door and see if he'd find any other residents or surprises.

"KEEP YOUR HEAD DOWN," Annalee warned as they neared the main road.

"Ow." Without asking permission, Theresa lay down on the seat and balanced her head against Anna's hip.

Once more Anna had to fight the surprise of being touched by a virtual stranger. But, whether she was distracted by driving or she'd acclimated to this girl who'd been in her life for two days, the disturbing sensation passed quicker this time. If she hadn't been so worried, she would have congratulated herself.

"Are you okay?" she asked for the tenth time.

"About the same. That bumpy road didn't help."

"We've got more bumps to come soon." With visions of Theresa giving birth on the front seat of her four-wheel drive, Anna drove fast yet carefully. She wouldn't feel calm until they had a second opinion on the pregnancy. Then, she'd already decided, if this Juney seemed alarmed by Theresa's condition or completely incompetent, she'd call Deputy Ben on his cell phone and have him meet them at the hospital.

They passed a few cars on the main road, but thankfully none of them were police cruisers. Before long, Anna was making the turn onto a gravel road marked with only a number and a letter, 87A. The road rose up the mountain like an undulating snake and by the second hard curve, Theresa roused herself.

"These curves are makin' me sick. I've got to sit up."

Anna slowed the truck and helped steady the girl until she was straight in the seat with one hand braced against the dash and the other against the door.

"How far is it?" she asked, a little out of breath.

Anna squinted ahead. "I honestly don't know. I heard she lived up near the top. I was hoping there would be a house close enough to the road to ask."

They passed a mailbox that had Route 3, Box 10 on it, but no name. A last name wouldn't have helped anyway. Anna hadn't heard the midwife's last name—only Juney. She searched for lights in the distance. Nothing but darkness.

As she drove on, the whole trip acquired the feeling of a wild-goose chase. What was she doing dragging this girl around these mountain roads when she could be in labor? Between the two of them they knew less about giving birth than most other women on the planet. Forty-eight hours ago Anna would have gleefully told anyone who asked that her life couldn't get much crazier. Well, today and tonight had outdone her wildest expectations.

Theresa drew in a sharp breath claiming Anna's attention. "I'm okay," she said before the question could be asked. "It's just a little car sickness."

Thinking to start a conversation and distract the girl, Anna said, "So, have you picked out a name for the baby?"

Theresa was silent for a moment, then she said, "No. I'm gonna leave that up to its new parents."

Startled, Anna forgot not to pry. "You're giving it up?"

"Yes, ma'am. As soon as my baby is born and I get it adopted into a safe place, then I can do what the police want me to do and testify." Anna saw Theresa remove her hand from the dash and rub her extended belly like an apology. "That's the only way I can keep Jimmy from killin' it."

The horror of giving up your baby to keep it alive didn't surprise Anna. She of all people, knew the sacrifices and hard choices women like herself and Theresa made every day, even if they did come from opposite ends of the economic spectrum. What surprised her was the girl's sense of calm.

She'd obviously lived with other hard choices and made her peace with her own pain. The choice to try to give her child a better future came naturally.

Run away, run away. Hide.

Anna frowned at the dark road. She would have fought back. If she had a child who was threatened by a nameless, or a well-known enemy, she'd hole up in a place like her cabin and fight whoever crossed the boundary intent on hurting them.

She understood the costs of fighting, though. She'd fought back for years in her own defense. But nothing had come of it. She'd gone through the police tests, the psychological tests. She'd told them everything she knew about the man. And in her opinion, she'd known more than any human female should have known. But the police hadn't helped. They'd taken her dress, the only thing she'd been wearing when she got away. They'd asked her a million questions, many of them over and over again. But none of it had helped. They'd never found him. He was still out there.

A chill ran through her. *Run away, run away. Think of something else.*

Up ahead, another mailbox loomed in the darkness. As they neared it, Anna saw the porch light of a house.

"Hallelujah," Anna breathed, for more reasons than one.

BEN STEPPED UP onto the porch expecting to be greeted by Anna's dogs, barking and snarling. When that didn't occur, he went for the obvious approach, in case someone might be inside. He knocked on the door.

Nothing.

He waited several minutes to give an occupant time to get to the door, or time to look through the peephole and decide it was safe enough to answer.

Nothing moved.

Ben propped a hand on the front window frame and casually leaned in to look through the glass. What he saw sent a prickling chill of danger through him and made him wish he'd been wearing his sidearm. He remained perfectly still.

Anna's dog, the big male, was standing on a trunk strategically placed near the window, staring at him with lethal intensity.

Ben blinked and the dog's hackles rose as he growled, showing more sharp teeth than Ben hoped ever to see up close again. The dog was so near his breath sent wisps of moisture to fog the glass. Thanking the stars for whoever had invented glass for windows, Ben slowly backed away.

His movement set the dog off and he barked, with a wild frenzy against the window. Ben remembered the dog snuffling around his boots when he'd been with Anna. Nothing friendly about him now. Police dogs were trained to bite and hold.

Something in the way Anna's dog had waited for him to make a move spoke to the fact that he was trained to do a little more than hold when he caught you. On foot, in the dark, Ben had no intention of testing whether that hundred pounds of assassin in fur knew he could come through the thin barrier of window glass in a heartbeat.

The smartest course was to leave and Ben had never been called dumb. Anna had chosen well again. But he regretted losing the opportunity to see a little more into her hidden life. Defeated but not deterred, he walked down the driveway until the barking tapered off. The moon hadn't risen yet, so he took out his flashlight and headed back to his camp.

MAYBE THE WOMAN WAS A WITCH after all. *Wouldn't that be ironic,* Anna thought as she watched the woman called Juney Bridger sit with her hands palm down on Theresa's belly. The midwife had been waiting for them at the road after they'd stopped lower down the mountain to ask directions.

When Theresa had asked her how she knew they were coming, she'd casually replied, "A neighbor called."

Now it was possible that the woman who had given them directions earlier might have called. And at the time, as Anna had thanked the neighbor, she'd asked her to do just that. The woman had laughed and replied, "Don't worry, she'll know."

Since they'd arrived and been ushered into a sturdy log cabin with braided rugs covering the pine floors and comfortable, locally made furniture, Juney had been preoccupied with Theresa. She hadn't asked who they were or how they'd found out about her. She'd settled Theresa into a lovely handmade rocking chair and fixed them all a warm cup of tea that tasted of lemon and an earthy mix of herbs. Now she seemed to be listening to Theresa's baby with her hands.

"This baby is coming soon," Juney said in a solemn voice. Then she smiled, "It's a sweet little girl." She looked from Theresa's belly to her eyes. "She says she'll be the first love of her momma's heart."

Tears spilled down Theresa's cheeks and Anna felt the sudden need to intervene. This baby couldn't be with her momma; she had to be hidden. "How soon?" she asked, then watched Juney cock her head as though she could hear a voice in the silence.

"Soon. This week, a few days. Hard to say because the moon is near full." As Juney Bridger said the word *moon,* she stared at Anna.

Anna couldn't stop herself from remembering. The blood looked black in the moonlight. Suddenly the image dispersed as though a cleansing wave had washed it out of her mind. Feeling unexpectedly lighter, Anna said, "Not tonight though."

"No," Juney said, and smiled. "But soon enough. Tonight was a little rehearsal." To Theresa she said, "How many babies did your mamma have?"

"Five," Theresa answered.

"Any trouble with the births? Any breech or with negative blood?"

"No, ma'am," Theresa replied. "Momma used to say having babies seemed to be the only thing she was good at. She sure wasn't good at lookin' out for the ones she brought into the world."

Juney patted her hand. "You're gonna be good at both. You just need to find a different man."

Theresa looked at Anna with wide eyes, but answered Juney. "Yes, ma'am."

"Bring her to me when her time comes," Juney said to Anna. "Night or day." Then to Theresa she said, "Will you be afraid to have me deliver you? Some folks call me a witch."

Theresa shook her head. "I'm not afraid. I feel better already."

"That's the tea. I'll give you some to take home. You can drink it anytime you feel wobbly like you did today."

There were two calmer women who left the midwife's cabin an hour later. Anna, always uncomfortable with strangers, felt no fear of this woman who looked like *Leave It To Beaver's* spry grandmother—even though she listened to the voices of the unborn and had waded into Anna's fears.

Most of her attention had been on Theresa, so Anna was surprised when Juney extended her hand for a parting handshake. She hesitated, fighting the habit of refusing to touch, to connect in any way with anyone, but the steady gaze of Juney Bridger won out.

As their hands clasped, Anna only felt warmth and friendliness, but Juney's smile disappeared. She placed her other hand over Anna's, making a sandwich, holding her captive.

"Run away, run away..." she whispered.

Anna started as if Juney had shouted her innermost thoughts. Which she had. She tried to pull her hand away, but the woman held her.

"You're strong," she said, gripping Anna's hand tighter with the word. "Strong enough to be knocked down and get up again." She nodded in approval. "What you don't know yet is, you're strong enough to start over, too." Juney loosened her hold and let Anna's hand slide from hers before smiling. "Thank you for bringing Theresa to me. I know it wasn't easy for you. I'll take good care of her." She waved to them as they went down the stairs. "I'll be seeing you again soon."

TRANSCRIPTION of taped session with female minor X, 15 years old. Excerpted from psychiatric evaluation of Dr. Antony Desillio, Ph.D., State of New York.

"Blood is black in the moonlight."

"His blood looked black?"

"Mine, too. It still feels black inside me."

"Will you tell me about what happened to you under the moon? I might be able to help you sort it out."

(Silence)

"Can you tell me how you got these cuts on your arms? Why your father found blood on your nightclothes this morning?"

"I was talking to the moon."

"The full moon? Last night?"

(Patient nodded)

"What did you talk about?"

"I asked to be invisible."

"And what did the moon say?"

"Nothing."

CHAPTER SIX

"WHAT'S THAT?" Theresa asked as Anna entered the room carrying milk and cookies. They'd made it safely back from their wild ride to Juney Bridger's, and Anna had high hopes of getting some food into Theresa before sending her to bed.

"It's a cello," Anna answered. She set the tray on the coffee table and crossed the room. Snapping the clasps, she opened the case and showed Theresa the instrument.

"It looks like a big violin," the girl said.

Anna slid her hand around the neck and pulled the instrument from the case. As always, the touch of the smooth cool neck and slight roughness of the strings sent a thrill of familiarity and calmness through her. This instrument had literally kept her alive in many ways. It was the one connection to the past she'd kept besides her real first name and her father's fortune. The cello had belonged to her mother.

"The sound is much deeper and fuller than a violin," Anna replied. "Remember the music you heard yesterday, on the CD? That was a cello and piano duet.''

Theresa ran her fingers along the well-worn bow that remained in the case. ''You play this, don't you?''

''Yes, I do,'' Anna said simply. Not mentioning the hours, the years she'd spent bending over her mother's cello in search of some kind of wisdom or peace. She'd learned that enriching old talents and learning new ones could fill the hours of her life almost as well as people might have, if she'd been born someone else. Or if she hadn't been chosen by him.

Anna started to place the instrument back in its velvet cradle when Theresa stopped her.

''Would you let me, let us—'' she touched her stomach ''—hear you play?''

Why not? Anna thought, then she realized somehow, even with her standoffishness and coldness, she and Theresa had bonded. She'd stopped feeling the girl's presence in her life like a thorn and had accepted a kindred spirit as a temporary roommate. And the girl seemed to have lost her fear of the Crazy Woman of Rain Mountain. Maybe if someone had taken the chance to help Anna when she'd been Theresa's age, things might have been different.

''I'll play while you eat,'' she said, motioning Theresa back to the couch.

As Anna settled into a rosewood chair and brought the instrument into position she had another epiphany. She'd felt different about Theresa and her situation after visiting Juney Bridger. Calmer. As if her feet were on an inevitable path she shared with Theresa. Her choices would be made and she would face what came with strength. Trusting a stranger, when so many who'd called themselves friends, had betrayed her, maybe she had gone round the bend.

Then the past and future slipped away as the rich notes of the cello filled the cabin like dark flowing honey. She would transport them both to somewhere safe, someplace like home. For a precious few moments, anyway.

A LITTLE AFTER SUNRISE, Ben's cell phone rang. He put down the branch he'd been using to prod the coals of the fire around the coffeepot, and answered, "Ravenswood."

"Hey, Ben."

"Sheriff."

"Picked up one other tidbit of information for you about that missing girl. And you're not gonna believe it 'cause I sure don't."

"What's that?"

"Well, one of her friends back in Elberton told a deputy that the girl is at least six months pregnant, maybe more. I think somebody's lying here.

A pregnant female couldn't outrun our deputies and search dogs.''

Ben didn't say so, but after what he'd seen the night before, he figured she had, and she'd made it to Annalee's. As unlikely as it seemed, the local recluse had taken her in. He wanted to be sure before he stirred up a hornet's nest though. He wouldn't want the law confronting Annalee if he could circumvent it.

"Oh, and one more thing. About Annalee Evans, as far as the computers can tell, she didn't exist before she moved here. No driver's license, no credit record, not even a parking ticket. Paid for the land in cash with a bank check out of New York. No other record of any kind. Strange, huh?''

THE SUN WAS HIGH ENOUGH to light the front windows of the cabin when Annalee checked on Theresa. Still asleep. Thinking to let the girl get caught up on the rest she'd missed on the run, Anna put the biscuits on the back of the stove to stay warm and decided to take the dogs out for a walk before breakfast. Hunter and Diva headed for the door as Anna pulled on her boots and picked up her shotgun. Always happy to be outside, they rushed through the opening in front of her. Hunter immediately became alert, growling menacingly. When she turned, Anna almost dropped the shotgun.

"You wouldn't shoot a man in a rocking chair, would you?"

Ben Ravenswood had made himself at home on her front porch. Still dressed in camouflage fatigues with his long legs and booted feet crossed in front of him, he looked like a tired extra from a war movie. Until you saw his face. Nothing tired about his steady gaze, and nothing friendly about the two-day growth of beard darkening his jaw. Hunter went into another round of growling and barked twice.

"Hunter, down," Anna ordered, more for Theresa's sake than Ben's. She didn't want to wake the girl and alarm her for no reason.

"Deputy Ben, you're beginning to wear on me," she said, trying to act like her normal self. But she'd lost her habitual hard front in the past few days. Theresa had softened her up. That was bad. Anna raised the shotgun, high enough to shoot the legs out from under him if he moved. "Do you have some kind of personality disorder? Or just a suicidal nature?"

BEN STARED PAST the shotgun and held Annalee's gaze. He had a better chance of talking his way into her cabin than by using force. She seemed different, even though her threatening words had sounded the same. More than concluding the case of the runaway witness, Ben just wanted to know

what was going on and why Annalee was involved.
If she had the girl inside, then the runaway had
gotten further with the Crazy Woman of Rain
Mountain than any other person in Wayne county
in the past five years.

Ben had to know how and why.

"Where is she, Annalee?"

Anna's arms shook slightly and she lowered the
gun. "Who?"

Ben made a move to sit up straighter, but Anna's
dog stood and growled in reaction. It looked as if
he would have to remain in the rocking chair until
Anna called off her guardians. "The girl. The runaway."

"I told you I—"

"I saw her last night."

Indignation straightened her back. "You've
been watching me, my cabin..." She reacted as
though he'd confessed to being some kind of pervert.

"It's my job, Anna. I followed her trail here."

"Well, she's gone. I took her to Chattanooga
last night. Arrest me if you want to, but you won't
find her now."

Ben watched her features for the hint of a lie.
Hard to say, she had that distancing, superior look
on her face. An expression that came from being
accused by an insignificant officer of the law, like
himself. Too stupid to live. Suddenly, sleeping on

the ground the past two nights made him grouchy, that and being held under the gun. He pushed to his feet.

He paid no attention to the growling dog less than a yard away. "I can have the sheriff up here with a search warrant and ten men in an hour. Is that what you want?"

The threat only made her expression more distant. "Then you better have several good lawyers, because if you try to harass me, I'll own this town. You've already trespassed at will on my land. You've been warned, haven't you? By rights I could shoot you and be done with it." Instead of aiming, however, she turned to go back inside.

"Anna, I'm only trying to help."

"You want to help?"

He nodded.

"Then go away and leave it be. The girl is gone."

BEN WATCHED THE ROAD for two hours before he gave up and drove into town. Maybe she had driven the girl out of the county. That would certainly fit her personality. What person within ten miles would take someone in who'd been delivered to their door by the Witch of Rain Mountain? No one. And, if the girl disappeared, certainly no one in Dalton Falls would waste a moment arguing the social conscience of Annalee Evans. They would more likely assume she'd murdered the girl and hung her remains in a tree to scare off poachers.

As was his habit, Ben waved to the clerk on his way to his office. He'd stopped by the house to shower and shave before coming in to make some kind of report. He wasn't ready to tell anyone about Annalee just yet. He had the distinct premonition that if he did, the sheriff would have a warrant and every available deputy on her front porch in a heartbeat. If for no other reason than to find out exactly what was going on up on Rain Mountain once and for all. It would supply the county gossips with enough ammunition to keep them at full speed for a year.

The thought of Anna's protected world being invaded for no good reason made his jaw tight. Ben wouldn't let that happen if he could help it. Even if keeping the information to himself for a while meant his job, he wasn't going to give her over just yet.

He made a report from an unidentified source that the girl, Theresa Smith, may have gotten a ride to Chattanooga and attached a lookout for local police just in case. Then he went over the computer printouts on Theresa and on Annalee.

THE CONFRONTATION WITH Ben Ravenswood, on her own front porch, had shaken Anna in more ways than one. First the sheer surprise that he could get so close to the house without the dogs or Anna herself detecting him. Then there were the lies she'd told him. In that she at least felt justified. Threatening her with a search warrant worried her a little, but what judge would believe she'd hide a fugitive? Certainly not one in Dalton Falls. She wasn't bluffing about lawyers, however. She had some of the best in the country on retainer and after the past years of major-league legal maneuvering they'd done for her, suing a small town in the Georgia mountains would seem like a fish-stick snack for a shark.

What really bothered her was realizing how great an effect Theresa was having on her well-planned, well-camouflaged persona. She hadn't realized that by making the decision to give a damn about what happened to the runaway and her baby, she'd opened up an inner part of herself she'd forgotten. Her solitary lifestyle had been fractured, and like Humpty Dumpty she wasn't sure it could be put back together again. Without warning, Theresa had thrust herself, along with Deputy Ben and the midwife Juney Bridger into Anna's life. And the baby was yet to come.

"What are we going to do?" Theresa asked in a worried voice.

Anna, interrupted by the source of her current predicament, almost smiled. "We wait for that baby. And you stay inside, away from the windows. I doubt if I scared Deputy Ben off for long.''

TRANSCRIPTION of taped session with female minor X, 15 years old. Excerpted from psychiatric evaluation of Dr. Antony Desillio, Ph.D., State of New York.

"Why do you wish to leave school?"

"I have to."

"I know there have been some security problems, but why leave? Won't you miss your friends?"

(Pause)

"They look at me like I'm crazy and talk about me like I'm deaf or retarded. No. I won't miss school."

"Isn't there one friend who has been nice to you? What about…"

(Rustling of paper)

"…Deanna?"

"She asked me if the bad man made me do sex stuff with him."

"What did you tell her?"

"I said that what he made me do was probably worse than sex."

"And what did he make you do?"

"Anything he wanted me to do. Anyway, the next day I got a note from Deanna's boyfriend asking if I wanted to meet him after school.

"No, Doctor, I won't miss my friends."

CHAPTER SEVEN

THE MOON WOKE ANNALEE.

The moon, shining through her window, whispering to the frightened child she had once been. *I can see you, no matter where you go.* Anna could never completely escape her memories because she could never escape the moon.

She pushed the covers aside and slid her arm into the bright block of light framed by the window. A shiver went through her as she slowly wiggled her fingers. No tape. Free. But still caught. She could make out the tiny lines of the scars just below her elbow.

The full moon. She'd tried to fight its pull, but the unexpected events this week had set her on edge. The old restlessness wouldn't let her win. She had to go. Quietly she slid out of bed and stood, then tugged her sleep shirt over her head.

Unselfconsciously naked, Anna moved through her dark cabin like a ghost, silent, purposeful. She collected the sharpest knife in the kitchen. Unafraid. She always fought putting her grown-up self aside and becoming…empty. Invisible. But once it happened, she would walk in another world, forgetting everything but the moon. She stopped at the couch, pulled on her boots and drew the Indian blanket throw around her bare shoulders before opening the front door.

Diva and Hunter whined to go with her but she ignored them. The pull of the moon was too strong. She was fourteen again, being led by a more powerful force. A few steps and she was outside in the light, headed for the top of the ridge and open sky.

BEN HAD BEEN HALF-ASLEEP in the makeshift surveillance blind he'd built in a thicket of mountain laurel when he noticed movement on Anna's front porch. He knew he had to be dreaming. It looked like Anna, wrapped in a blanket, long dark hair flowing down her back in a loose tangle. The moonlight was too bright to be mistaken. It was Anna and, as he focused his binoculars, he realized that her legs were bare. He remembered admiring those long legs in town, but watching her go out in the woods alone, without her dogs and half-dressed sent an eerie shimmer of unease up his spine. Wally's words came back to him in a rush.

I heard she walks in the woods under the full moon, naked as a newborn.

Even though Ben had been watching the house to find the girl, there was no way he could leave this puzzle unsolved. There were a few legitimate reasons for Anna to be out. After all, it was her land, her home. Maybe a plumbing problem had sent her to the woods to answer the call of nature. Having spent the past few nights away from home and conventional bathroom facilities, he could appreciate the necessity of a walk in the woods. But as she moved farther than she needed to go to accomplish a simple bodily function, Ben swore under his breath.

Using every skill he'd learned as a hunter and tracker he followed Annalee. He wasn't afraid of being shot if he spooked her. He was afraid of never knowing her secrets. Catching him on her property one more time would mean more than a simple lawsuit. It would mean war. And the last thing he wanted to do was fight with Annalee.

As he watched, she hiked up the ridge just south of her cabin with a wooden-stepped sort of purpose. When she pushed straight through a thicket instead of going around, the thought occurred to him that she might be sleepwalking.

Or meeting a lover, in a hurry.

Thunderstruck by the thought, Ben followed, keeping in sight. Even if it killed him, he had to know.

She reached the top of the ridge and moved directly to the center of the highest point, where a small clearing allowed the moonlight to shine brightly on the ground. Standing in the luminance, Anna raised her face to the moon.

Ben could barely breathe and the ache in his chest made his ears ring. The stillness in the dark around him felt unfriendly, as if telling him that watching Annalee was against the rules. She had a right to her secrets. But he couldn't help it, he had to see...

Annalee, after saying what looked like a silent prayer to the moon, levered off her boots. Then, before Ben could decide what might happen next, and what he should do about it, she swung the blanket from her shoulders and let it drift to the ground.

She was naked.

He decided in that moment that the vision of the two deer in the moonlight, which he'd thought of as the most beautiful thing he'd ever seen, had just been outdone.

By the Crazy Woman of Rain Mountain.

ANNA COULD FEEL THE MOONLIGHT on her skin, even though the doctors had said she couldn't. They'd insisted it was all in her mind. But she knew better. She didn't want to feel it, but what she wanted had never seemed to matter.

She straightened the corners of the blanket and sat down in the middle. Time to be invisible. She brought the knife up and let the brilliant full moon

shine along the sharp edge. The image of the bad
man twisted in the back of her thoughts. His words,
The moon makes you invisible.

She hadn't wanted to believe him. But he'd been
right. In the four months he'd kept her, he'd made
her invisible. No one had ever found her, not the
police, not her father. She'd been forced to run
away on her own. Now, like other nights when the
moon was full, she had to make herself invisible
to him.

With little regard for the pain, Anna stretched
out her arm and made a clean, shallow cut next to
the scar of a former cut. For a moment, she thought
she'd heard an intake of breath close to her. She
looked to her right, then up at the moon. It must
have been her own breath, her own pain, yet she'd
felt nothing. A tiny sting, no more. She put the
knife aside and wet her finger with the drops of
blood welling from her skin, and began marking.

Forehead, chest, shoulder to shoulder. A bas-
tardized form of the sign of the cross. The blood
looked black in the moonlight. The bad man had
marked her with his own blood, after he'd tied her
down like a sacrifice and covered her mouth with
duct tape. The memory of the chemical smell and
taste of the tape rushed at her from the darkness,
making her gag as it used to do in her dreams. She
swallowed and forced the phantom away.

Run away, run away. Hide.

She had the power now. She'd never be taped or tied again. Her own blood would make her invisible, her own watchfulness would keep her safe. The moon had become her guardian, not her captor's. And wherever he was, looking up at the same moon, she willed him to feel her absence.

To complete the ceremony, she marked her belly and each of her knees, then she stretched out on the blanket so the moon could find her.

IT HAD TAKEN EVERY BIT of Ben's professional training for him to remain still when he'd seen the knife. Any fleeting fantasies of beautiful wood nymphs running naked through the trees had gone right out of his head as the moon reflected off the raised blade. He'd watched the first cut with heart-pounding alarm and decided there wouldn't be a second one. But as he'd stood to intrude and intercept the knife, she'd put it down.

Now watching her complete whatever ritual she'd begun, Ben had to face the fact that he was completely out of his depth here. He'd held the quaint opinion that Annalee Evans couldn't be as dangerous or as strange as the people in town said. He'd decided in his heart that she was merely a lonely woman who'd probably been hurt by a man in the past. He'd even been willing to accept it, if a man had been waiting for her in the clearing. But there had been no friendly, loving face to greet her, only the pale, cold moon.

Her skin looked like smooth, white marble in the moonlight, her hair bluish black, and Ben imagined she would be cool to the touch. But all around her, where there wasn't moonlight, there was darkness. A darkness beyond anything he'd considered. What had driven Annalee to the top of a mountain? To the solitary life of a recluse, and true lunacy.

His grandmother used to call it moon-sickness, or the people afflicted, moon-walkers. Hundreds of old mountain legends were intertwined with the moon and its powers, from the Indian claims of moon people, to the pioneers planting certain crops under the proper phase, to the drought of 1969 after the first real moon walk took place.

He had no idea how far into the netherworld of moonlight Annalee had gone, though he knew anything with blood involved was not done on a lark. It took a certain amount of belief and commitment to stomach the spilling of blood for a ritual. Standing over her, he almost expected a ghost, or an animal familiar, or another type of portent to drift out of the surrounding shade. His ears were so attuned to the silence, he thought he could hear the moonlight sizzle on the leaves and on the Crazy Woman of Rain Mountain like the drizzling winter rain that had named this place.

Then he heard a scream.

The sound had come from behind him, echoing up the hill from Annalee's cabin. He watched as Annalee sat bolt upright then froze like a wary deer smelling the air.

The clanging of what sounded like pots and pans combined with the wild barking of dogs, sending up a racket that couldn't be ignored. Before he could react, Annalee sprang to her feet, yanked on her boots and ran directly toward him. He'd stupidly taken up a position between her and the cabin. Without time to move, he caught her as she ran straight into his arms.

He braced for her to scream and fight. Instead of fighting, however, she went motionless. He could feel cool skin and the fast pounding of her heart.

DON'T SCREAM, Annalee's mind instructed. *If you scream, he'll tape your mouth.* She didn't move, didn't speak. Invisible. A man's arms were around her. She could smell familiar scents of wood smoke and soap—calming scents, not like him. No cigarettes, no tape, no blood.

"Annalee, it's me, Ben." When she didn't answer, he loosened his arms. "Deputy Ben, remember?"

Anna looked up into the man's face, half in shadow, half in light, and thought she knew him.

The fear eased, she did know him. But her mind was on the moon, in the past, Ben's features seemed to be obscured by the mist of distance.

The noise from the cabin crescendoed again, and Anna responded to the frantic call for help. She pushed at his chest. "Let me go! I have to go!" She'd forgotten the girl's name, she'd forgotten why, but she knew she had to protect the girl in the cabin from something. Someone.

As Anna pushed away from him, Ben grabbed her wrist to stop her. "Wait." Holding her with one strong hand, he ripped open his shirt with the other, sending buttons flying like bullets. One of them struck her in the chest and she realized she was still naked. No time to be normal now and blush. He yanked his shirt off and half forced half helped it on her. "You don't know what's down there."

Wearing his shirt and her own boots, Annalee set off in an all-out run for the cabin. It was downhill, and in several places she slipped. Each time, she felt Ben's strong arm steady her. He seemed to be all around her, in the scent from his shirt, the cadence of his breath as they ran, the crash of two pairs of boots through the underbrush.

They reached the moon-washed porch at the same time. It was Ben, however, who shoved the front door open and stumbled inside first.

ALL HELL BREAKING LOOSE couldn't describe
Ben's take on what happened next. The first un-
happy surprise was the one-hundred-pound dog
that launched itself at his chest. In very short order
he was on the floor with the air knocked out of
him, staring into the growling maw of his old
buddy the male Doberman, without the slight ben-
efit of window glass between them, while the female barked in support.

The girl was on the couch, crouched over and
surrounded by pots and pans, spoons and spatulas.
She'd obviously been the one making all the noise.
She dropped the pan and meat hammer when she
saw Annalee.

"It's the baby!" she wailed, then had to stop
and pant. "The baby's coming!" A low moan escaped her.

Another growl rumbled through the dog.

"Hunter, Diva, come!"

Suddenly the weight left his chest and Ben gingerly sat up, no worse for wear other than a few
scratches and welts on his bare skin. He glanced
at Anna, expecting her usual sarcasm, but she
seemed frozen, confused.

"You've got to help me..." the girl pleaded.
When there was no answer and the pain eased, the
girl stared at Annalee. "What's wrong with you?"
she asked, the beginnings of true fear coloring her
gaze.

Ben watched as Anna, with obvious effort, tried to pull herself together. She gathered his shirt in one hand and ran the other through her hair, dislodging two leaves. She turned her silence in his direction like a question.

"We need to take her to the hospital," Ben said, keeping his voice as calm and normal as he could after the last headlong dive into Anna's strange life.

"No. No hospital!" The girl insisted. Tearful eyes looked to Annalee. "You promised to take me to Juney. You promised."

Whether it was the word *promise* or the odd name of another alleged witch that got through, Anna shook off her strange trancelike state.

"I'll take you. Let me get dressed."

Then she was gone, leaving Ben with the girl he'd spent five long days searching for. "My name's Ben," he said, trying to look harmless even though he was half-dressed and bloody from the race through the woods and the dog's attack.

"I know who you are," she said, then sucked in a long breath.

"You know we have to take you to a hospital if your baby is coming."

She shook her head. Case closed. Before he could argue, Annalee returned fully dressed in khaki pants and a plaid shirt. She handed his shirt back to him and, without looking him fully in the eyes, said, "Sorry about the buttons and the blood. I'll buy you another."

Then she leaned over the girl on the couch. "Can you stand up?"

"I think so. But I'm all wet. The water broke."

"Wait a second." Again Annalee left the room. She returned with a towel and what looked like a baggy dress over her arm. He didn't have time to see much because she ordered him to turn around.

"Let's put this on. Those jeans won't do you any good anyhow," she said to the girl.

They were the kindest words Ben had ever heard from Annalee Evans and for a brief moment he envied this pregnant teenager. She'd obviously gotten to the Crazy Woman of Rain Mountain on a level Ben had never even approached. Her urgency had even called Anna back from whatever foreign territory her mind had been wandering. Had called her back from the moon.

A moment later, they moved up next to him with Anna supporting the girl. "Will you open the door?" Anna asked.

Having used the last of his patience with the changing of clothes, he turned and lifted Theresa easily into his arms. "You open the door," he ordered Anna.

The dogs followed them to the porch where Anna immediately ordered them to stay. Ben carried the girl to the passenger side of Anna's truck,

but when he tried to get in, Theresa insisted that
Anna sit next to her. Anna's tense grip on his arm
claimed his complete attention. He couldn't remember if she'd ever willingly touched him before, but he thought not.

"If I let you drive, you have to swear to go
where I tell you. No hospital, no police."

When he hesitated, she released him and walked
toward the driver's side. No debate. He caught her
at the front of the truck and turned her toward him.

"I'm not letting you do this alone," he said.

"Yes or no. Will you go where I say?"

He looked down at her resolute face in the
moonlight and saw a smear of blood on her forehead. He wanted to rub the blood off and tell her
she never had to be afraid again. In that moment,
he would have killed for her without ever knowing
why. She had to be a witch.

"Yes. Where you say."

JUNEY BRIDGER MET THEM at the door along with
a woman and a young man. After introducing them
as her daughter, Sarah Liam, and son Roy, she sent
Roy off on an errand while she instructed Ben to
bring Theresa inside.

"Follow Sarah. Take her in the back, through
that door."

Anna followed, watching Ben maneuver Theresa's burdened body with surefooted ease. It felt

good to let someone help. She'd been fighting every battle alone for so long. Tonight, between the moon, and Ben and Theresa, she felt as though all the strength had been drained from her body.

"Put her in the rocker, there," Juney said, then turned to Annalee before she could enter the room. Without asking permission, Juney licked her own thumb and rubbed the smear of blood from Anna's forehead like a mother might tidy up a child. Too tired to stop her, Anna simply watched the expression on the midwife's face.

"You did good tonight," she said. "You got her here." Then with a pat on her cheek, Juney repeated, "You did good."

Becoming all business, Juney moved forward to shoo Ben out of the room. He seemed transfixed by the hot tub that took up most of the space. "It's the Swedish method," Juney said as she faced Ben's incredulousness. "My ladies give birth in water. Soothes the pull of gravity—" she glanced at Anna "—especially during the full moon."

Looking unconvinced, Ben stopped next to Annalee before he left the room. "In water?" he asked, then shook his head.

"Both of you make yourself at home. Roy will bring you some tea. I'll call when the time comes."

In a tired trance, Anna followed Ben into the living room she'd seen the evening before. The big comfortable rocker had been moved to the birthing room. So, without thinking, she found herself sitting on the roomy, quilt-covered couch next to Ben. She couldn't seem to shake the tiredness. If she'd ever believed in fairy tales, she would swear the sandman had visited her.

Roy entered the room from some other part of the cabin and brought them a porcelain pot of hot tea, two cups and several slices of lemon. He left them after asking, as quaintly as Juney herself, whether they needed something to eat. She and Ben both declined, but, since Roy had gone to the trouble of pouring them each a cup, they decided to try the tea.

"You know we should have taken her to the hospital," Ben said a few moments later. He glanced at the closed door to the birthing room. "We may still have to take her."

Too tired for any sort of alarm, Anna told him the truth. "She can't be found until she has the baby and puts it up for adoption."

"Why? I told you she's wanted as a witness. She's not a fugitive. Not in the strictest sense."

"If she testifies, the boyfriend will kill her baby."

Ben shook his head. "She'd be under police protection. We can protect her better than you can up there in that cabin."

Anna felt a chill like a breath of winter insinuating itself around a window frame. Cold and alone. She knew about police protection. That and one nosy neighbor could get you on the front page of the newspaper, or dead.

"No, you can't," Anna said then suddenly yawned. She couldn't think about it right now. No fear, no making of plans, no defenses. Only sleep. She felt Ben's arm slide around her, then found herself resting against him. "No, you can't," she said, or thought she said.

"Go to sleep," Ben's low voice whispered in her ear.

ANNA WOKE UP several hours later feeling warm and protected and absolutely without fear. Eyes still closed, she stretched and found she was tangled in the blankets or twisted in the sheets because her arms were weighted down. Without alarm she squirmed experimentally and the weight moved, accompanied by a sigh.

Annalee Evans slowly opened her eyes and looked into the sleeping features of Ben Ravenswood. There was no confusion. She recognized where she was and wondered how she'd ended up on the couch wrapped in the arms of the man who'd seemed to be dogging her boot heels for the past week. Or the past six months if truth be told.

She finally had him exactly where she wanted him. Close enough for her to examine and memorize but sound asleep so she wouldn't have to push him away, or explain herself, or protect herself.

He'd seen her in the woods, deep in her rituals with the moon. He'd seen her naked, given her his shirt without questions or lectures.

Now it was her turn to look.

She stared at his nose, strong and masculine, and wished for a fleeting moment that his eyes were open so she could see the clear hazel color tinted by humor. Her fingers itched to trace the arch of his eyebrows, the high slash of his cheekbones and the mystifying shape of his mouth. His lips were full and, she knew, quick to smile. She slowly drew one arm from under his and he shifted but didn't wake up. With one shaking finger, she touched his full bottom lip.

He brushed his hand over his mouth and turned away in such a childlike gesture that Anna smiled. If she sat down to calculate the last time she'd really smiled, she'd probably cry. Too long.

She touched the bump of thread where his top button used to be, before he'd sacrificed it for her, and felt a rush of gratitude and something else— contentment. She spent another few moments enjoying the weight, the smell, the comfort of him. The gift of that was more than she'd ever expected. Then with careful, slow movements, she withdrew from Ben's protective embrace on the couch. She'd worry later about why his closeness, so over-whelmingly male, hadn't kept her from sleeping happily in his arms. Perhaps it had been the tea. Perhaps it had been the man.

Tiptoeing across the room, Anna carefully opened the door to the birthing room. She wanted to check on Theresa. Without looking up, Juney motioned for Anna to enter. Leaning back in the hot tub, Theresa seemed to be asleep, as well, or so relaxed she didn't need to move. The midwife was seated opposite her on the side of the tub, presumably in baby-catching position. Her daughter, Sarah, was seated in a chair behind her.

At Juney's wave, Anna moved to the opposite side of the girl and touched her shoulder. "How are you doing?" she asked, keeping her voice low.

Theresa's eyes fluttered open, and she reached one wet hand to take Anna's. "It's not so bad," she said, sounding faraway. "But I feel like a prune." She moved one finger to demonstrate the wrinkles in her waterlogged skin.

"Are you ready to push again?" Juney asked.

Theresa nodded.

"All right, on the next contraction, push," Juney instructed. To Anna she said, "We're almost there. She's doing just fine."

Noticing the absence of clocks in the room, Anna asked, "What time is it?"

"A little after five. She'll deliver with the sun.

That usually means a boy, but in this case it'll be a headstrong little girl.''

The sun had been up an hour when Theresa's daughter was placed in Anna's arms.

"But I—" Anna protested, ready to plead total inexperience.

Juney's daughter, Sarah Liam, just laughed, sounding much like her no-nonsense mother. "Don't worry. She won't break."

Anna looked down into the tiny, scrunched face of the newest citizen of Dalton Falls, Georgia, and felt something deep and strong move inside her. The protective, animal instinct she'd studied in books was a poor relation to the devotion she was experiencing. Anna knew about the many bad things that could befall this child, but gazing at the baby's tiny hand fisted against her own downy cheek, she swore that this one would not be hurt. No bad man would touch her, including her father.

"She looks like a baby squirrel I found in the woods once," Ben said as he peeked over Anna's shoulder.

Anna, ready to defend, quickly turned on him. "What?"

"The squirrel had a little more hair though."

He laughed in the face of her outrage and Anna had to catch her breath. Everything was happening too fast. How could so much have changed that she wanted to kiss this laughing man, to stay in this houseful of people who welcomed life, and to protect the child in her arms with the considerable means at her disposal?

Shaken, Anna couldn't speak. If she tried she might burst into tears, and, as she'd found out years before, tears were a weakness. They clouded your vision so you couldn't move on.

"What's her name?" Ben asked, trying to make amends, she supposed.

"The mama wouldn't pick a name," Sarah said before Anna could reply. "Wouldn't say why."

"I know why," Anna said. Belatedly making up her mind about getting involved, she took the baby to her mother.

Resting in the guest room in a big, comfortable-looking bed, Theresa looked a little pale but much better than Anna would have expected after the ordeal of the previous few days. Anna sat down next to her with the baby in her arms.

"You did a fine job, Theresa. She's a beautiful little girl."

Theresa stared at Anna, rather than the baby, with a kind of non-expression on her face. Anna pushed on.

"What are you going to name her?"

"I told you. Her real parents get to name her." Theresa shifted her attention to the bedspread, to her feet, anywhere but the baby.

Anna found a mother's voice inside herself.

"Theresa, this is your baby, do you want her or not?"

Fat tears rolled down the girl's cheeks as she stared at Anna. "You know I can't—he'll hurt her."

"Listen to me. He can't hurt her. I can make you and the baby disappear. I have the money and I have the lawyers. You can have a new name, move to a new place and start over. He'll never find you. The only thing you have to do is never come home."

Theresa stared at her in numb confusion. "How can I—" Then she scanned Anna's features. "You're not really crazy, are you?"

Anna didn't even blink at the question. After all, the girl had seen her half-naked and marked with blood. *Run away, run away. Hide.* No, she didn't believe she was crazy. Not right now anyway. "You don't have to know anything. And, no, I'm not crazy. I'm an expert at becoming someone else." The baby squirmed, causing Anna to shift her in her arms.

"Someone is chasing you," Theresa said, comprehension dawning.

"He was, but I don't know anymore. It's been fourteen years." She sighed and squeezed Theresa's hand. "But he never found me. And Jimmy won't find you if we work together. Now rub those tears out of your eyes and look at me."

Theresa used the sheet to dry her cheeks.

"If you want this baby more than living in Georgia, more than seeing your family or friends ever again, then take her and name her." She held out the baby. "I'll see that you get a whole new start."

Theresa's tears made new tracks down her face but she held out her arms for her baby. Before Anna could leave, Theresa grabbed her hand. "The first time I saw you, I knew you would help me. I just didn't know how much. Thank you."

Feeling better than she had in a very long time, now that decisions had been made and a plan of action chosen, Anna smiled. At that moment, the baby started to cry.

"She's probably hungry," Theresa said. "But I don't know exactly what to do."

Knowing when to defer to the experts, Anna turned to go get Sarah. That's when she found Ben Ravenswood standing in the doorway.

TRANSCRIPTION of taped session with female minor X, 15 years old. Excerpted from psychiatric evaluation of Dr. Antony Desillio, Ph.D., State of New York.

"Your father says he's never seen you cry. Why is that? You must be sad sometimes."

"Crying doesn't do any good. It doesn't stop anything from happening, and it doesn't make it feel better later."

"It's normal to cry when you're hurt."

"I cried at first. But then I learned, tears make you stupid and weak. The bad man taught me that."

"The bad man isn't here to see you if you cry now."

"No, but everyone else is. They all want to see."

CHAPTER EIGHT

AT JUNEY'S INSISTENCE, they left Theresa in the guest room with Sarah and the new baby. In the living room Ben pulled the midwife aside and explained the importance of keeping Theresa's presence a secret, at least until she'd recovered enough to be taken for an interview with the sheriff.

"Now, Deputy Ben," Juney Bridger said, placing her hands on her hips. "Have you ever heard me or mine telling tales around this one-horse town?"

Ben had to smile. Usually the tales had been told about them not by them. "No, ma'am. I just need to know she won't be bothered till I can put together a likely story for my boss about why I didn't bring her in."

She studied him closely. "You're not worried about a boss or a job. You need to look out after our Annalee."

Thinking the woman had read his mind, because he was in a hurry to talk to Anna about what he'd overheard her say to Theresa, he agreed. "That's my plan if she'll let me."

Juney reached for his hand, cocked her head then added, "First she will, then she won't. Justice won't save her. You'll know what to say when the time comes." She smiled as if what she'd said had made perfect sense and released his hand. "It's the light she's afraid of, not the dark. She knows the dark."

"WHO ARE YOU THEN, really?"

Anna had been waiting for the question, or questions, ever since she and Ben had gotten into the truck. She'd allowed him to drive, thinking he might put off the interrogation until they got back to the cabin, but he'd only waited until they reached the main road.

"It doesn't matter anymore," Anna answered, feeling as distant from the other fearful, suspicious Annalee as she ever had. She didn't want to go back, not yet.

"It matters to me."

"Why? Because you're a policeman and policemen ask questions?" She couldn't help showing her contempt. All the policemen, all the questions she'd answered, and still they'd never found the man who'd taken her. And she'd had to run.

"No. Because I'm a man and—" he turned to look at her "—I want to know you."

He wanted to know her. Anna dragged her gaze from his and stared out the window of the truck.

Why? Her mind shifted through memories of the night before: Ben running down the mountain beside her, Ben carrying Theresa and driving her to Juney's, waking up on the couch in Ben's arms. She glanced at him sideways.

He couldn't be one of those who thrived on prying into people's well-structured lives until they found the awful secret that would tear the house down. Her protective instincts wouldn't believe it. He couldn't be.

"My real name is Annalee Winters." It had been so long since she'd spoken that name aloud she was surprised it came out sounding normal. Just the way it used to when she'd been that person. When Ben didn't react, she faced him.

"And..." he prodded. He obviously didn't recognize the name.

"And a long time ago I was kidnapped."

Ben was silent for several moments. In the interim, he turned the truck onto the gravel road leading up Rain Mountain toward Anna's driveway. Then he asked, "What happened?"

What happened? That's what everyone had wanted to know, the police, her father, the doctors and especially the press. She'd talked voluntarily to the police and reluctantly to the doctors, but rarely to her high-profile, guilt-ridden father, and to the press, not at all.

But unlike the police and the doctors and her

father, the press hadn't given up. They'd bribed three housekeepers and several of her neighbors. They'd followed her to school and home again, interviewing her teachers and other students. They'd christened her the most famous kidnap victim since Patty Hearst and the Lindbergh baby, and until she'd dropped out of sight using another identity, she'd been a virtual prisoner on her father's Connecticut estate until his death.

And he, the bad man, was still out there somewhere. Searching as he'd warned her he would if she ever left him.

Run away, run away. Hide. If she broke her silence now, he might come and find her as he'd promised. She knew enough about him to know he'd never give up.

Anna braced herself as Ben maneuvered the truck through the deep ruts in the road. "Do you want to know what happened, or just what he did to me?" She couldn't soften the snide tone of voice. In the beginning she'd thought people wanted to know to help. But it turned out most only wanted to know...to know. For their own dark, private reasons.

Ben stepped on the brake at the top of Anna's driveway and by sheer will forced her to look at him. "I want to know whatever you want to tell me," he said. But his eyes said everything.

Anna sighed. Everything and nothing. Telling

Ben couldn't help her after so many years of silence, but knowing him had helped her. The past few days had changed her, she hoped for the better, and she owed him for that. She'd discovered a new aspect of herself and the outside world and in return she'd tell him what she could.

"Let's go back to the cabin. I'll fix us some breakfast."

THE DOGS MET THEM on the porch.

Since Ben had arrived in Anna's truck, with Anna, they paid little attention to him. They seemed to be more intent on their master and their next meal.

"I'll put a pot of coffee on," Anna said, once they were in the door. Then she paced toward the back of the cabin with the dogs on her heels, leaving him standing near the entrance. She seemed more uncomfortable having him in her house than she'd been alone with him in the closer confines of the truck.

Ben could understand her nervousness in this situation. If she'd been hurt in the past, then inviting a man his size and a virtual stranger into her cabin out here in the middle of the woods took an extraordinary amount of courage. But then she had to be stronger than people might assume, to live such a solitary life. Most folks couldn't take much of being alone.

Rather than finding a seat, Ben used the opportunity to walk around the room and see what he'd wanted to see for a long time. Anna's home.

The cabin was well built, log-to-log, no chinking, but he already knew that from the outside. He walked over to the wall-sized fireplace at one end of the living room and ran a hand along the stonework. River rock, hand-placed with a firebox big enough to heat the cabin nicely if the power failed. Again, as with everything, Anna had planned well for disaster. There was even an iron hook that would swing out and hold a cooking pot over the fire.

He studied the heavy oak mantel and its contents before shaking his head in wry amusement. Most folks would have decorated with pictures of family or friends, maybe some flowers. Anna's held a large, perfectly shaped pinecone, a small silver bowl filled with what looked like possum teeth, two fat beeswax candles and an assortment of delicate feathers arranged around the skull of a deer. It looked more like a pagan altar than a shelf over the fireplace. The Witch of Rain Mountain. The only things missing were eye of newt and maybe some rattlesnake rattles. The vision of Anna in the moonlight with a bloody knife crowded his thoughts. Her rituals…he'd get to that. He'd ask her. But not yet. He turned to face the living room.

The furniture was deceptively simple, classic designs in expensive woods. Not showy but painstakingly crafted, and well beyond the means of ninety-eight percent of the citizens in Dalton County. That didn't surprise him. Living in a cabin didn't necessarily mean poverty. And certainly Annalee Evans had never given the impression of being poor.

Crazy, maybe, but not poor.

Ben spotted the large antique trunk Anna's dog had used to climb on and scare the bejeezus out of him the other night. It seemed so innocuous in the daylight, sitting by the door with a pink-and-white quilt draped over it.

Then he saw the cello.

Now there was an instrument you didn't find every day in the mountains. The case was scuffed, but it had a brass plate engraved with an elaborate *W.* He made a mental note to ask Anna about it later. He wanted to know everything, yet he didn't want her to feel she was under a microscope. This wasn't a police investigation, it was personal.

He could hear her talking to the dogs in the kitchen. Again, hearing her almost loving tone of voice made something inside him ache. Ben ran a hand over his face. *You've dropped pretty low when you're jealous of a dog, old sport. Maybe you've been on your own a couple of years too long.*

To derail his train of thought, he crossed the

Oriental rug to the alcove with built-in bookshelves from ceiling to floor. In the center of the space sat a large, finely made cherry-wood desk, but it was obvious this room had been built for books; hundreds of them, maybe even thousands. He scanned some of the titles and again felt out of his depth. Anna's library appeared better endowed than the two university libraries he'd been acquainted with. There were books filed by the Dewey decimal system, on a range of subjects. He was reading off the tenth title, *Small Animal Husbandry,* under Veterinary Science when Anna appeared next to him with a cup of coffee.

He took the cup from her. "Thank you."

"I put some cream in it, do you want sugar?"

"No, this is great." He stopped her before she could walk away. "Did you go to veterinary school?"

"No," she answered. "I studied at home."

Ben took a sip of his coffee and watched Anna return to the kitchen. Studied at home? Was there any part of Annalee Evans/Winters that could be considered normal? She seemed well educated yet had a makeshift altar on one side of the room facing a wall stuffed with science textbooks. And here he stood, firmly in the middle. Would he ever find the real Anna? Would she give him that much time?

He prowled among her books another twenty

minutes smelling bacon and biscuits, cooking before she appeared with a tray.

"Come on, let's sit outside," she said.

As he opened the door for her, he watched her gaze touch the shotgun positioned by the entrance. Then she glanced at him.

"Do you want it?" he asked, perfectly willing to take the tray and let her have her protection. She didn't need it with him, although he figured she wasn't sure of that yet.

Slowly she shook her head. "No, not today."

"I WAS FOURTEEN YEARS OLD," Anna said in a low, calm voice.

They'd finished breakfast and were now sitting in rockers, drinking coffee, and Ben was trying to get into the past. He couldn't say why, but knowing about Anna, past and present, had become an obsession. Juney Bridger had been right. He didn't care about his boss or his job, other than keeping Theresa out of trouble. Everything else about him was tangled up in Anna.

"He took me out of a parking lot at the mall. One moment I was with my friends, the next I was…" Her voice trailed off and she took a sip of coffee. "Trap—" Anna's voice broke and she cleared her throat. "Trapped."

Ben watched her, feeling helpless. He was sitting too far away to touch her for encouragement, and Anna probably wouldn't have allowed it anyway. She'd withdrawn back into the distance she used to keep the world at bay. The closeness he thought they'd found in the past twenty-four hours seemed to have been a hallucination.

"He took me somewhere upstate—I don't know where exactly—and kept me locked in a room with no windows."

Ben was beginning to get the heebie-jeebies. He'd been around all kinds of crime and criminals. He'd take a straightforward assault or crime of passion any day over the murky, mostly unexplainable actions of a serial criminal. If Anna had been taken to a special place that had been prepared ahead of time, the man who took her had most likely done that kind of thing before. She hadn't been the first or most probably the last. The thought made his stomach uneasy.

He couldn't hold his next question inside, he had to know. "Did he rape you?"

Anna held his gaze steadily. "No. Not the way you mean. He called me his little girl." She looked away and went on as if to hurry and get the questions over with. "I was only fourteen, but I know my age was no protection. Sometimes he would touch me, in ways men touch women, and then do things to himself. When I'd start to cry, he'd get angry and leave me alone for a few days. Alone in the room with no food or water. I never knew if he was coming back or not." She drew in a deep breath of air as though talking about it made it hard to breathe. A sad smile twisted her mouth, "My doctor said he was conflicted."

She went on as though she had no choice, her voice fading, growing dull and childlike. "He used to brush my hair on the good days, and polish my nails." Anna looked down at her hands and wiggled her unadorned fingers. "On the bad days— the days of the full moon—he would tape my hands and ankles. My m-mouth—"

Ben had heard enough. This wasn't an investigation, there was no reason to make her relive it. His curiosity, even though based in concern, wasn't worth the mental anguish he could see in Anna's face. He left his chair and squatted in front of hers. He took her hands in his, holding lightly so as not to scare her. Then he reached up and brushed the tears off her face with his knuckles.

"Shh—don't. You don't have to tell me any more."

Anna looked down at him for several heartbeats without recognition, yet rested her hands in his. She was winded, as if she'd struggled through quicksand.

"I haven't told you about the moon," she said finally.

No, she hadn't. He remembered all too well how

she'd looked naked in the moonlight and how he'd flinched when she'd picked up the knife.

"I know it's important, and I want to know. But you can tell me another time, okay?"

He stood and slowly pulled her to her feet. With his hands on her arms he held her and stared into her faraway gaze. She was looking at him, but not, and he couldn't stand the absence for another moment. Not after having been included in small parts of her life.

He rubbed her arms as if to warm her. "Come back, Annalee."

He watched her frown in effort and brought one hand up to cup her chin. "I'm right here, Anna, it's Ben."

Something like humor flickered deep in her brown eyes. "I know who you are." The frozen look faded. "You're the trespasser who won't mind the signs."

Ben laughed except he felt like crying, or punching the man who'd hurt her. "Yeah, that would be me." Without waiting or thinking, he pulled her to his chest and hugged her firmly. "Good to have you back," he said into her hair. "I've been waiting for you."

SEVERAL HOURS LATER, after Ben had left, Anna sat down on the couch in a quandary. Now that she had her house to herself again, she didn't know what to do in it. She'd swept and mopped and dusted the books. She'd gone through paperwork and made a list of the steps to take regarding Theresa and her daughter and their new lives. She and the dogs had hiked up to the ridge top to retrieve the blanket and kitchen knife she'd used to greet the full moon.

Her life was tidy and contained once more. Although, after having grumbled through the past few days of unexpected excitement, she missed the tumult of having Theresa in the cabin.

And she missed Ben.

Anna had gone over everything she could remember having been said between them and found that her first instincts had been right. She did trust him and he'd proven he was a man of his word. So far. She'd stepped out on a limb by telling him more about her true self than she'd told any one person in more than five years. In the other instances, her trust had been misplaced and she'd been taught an unpleasant lesson over and over again. She hoped in Ben's case, he would prove the exception. Not only because she didn't want to have to pull up stakes and disappear one more time, but because for once she wanted to believe in someone.

Whether it was the ancient pull of man to woman, which had been so absent from her life, or the steady dependability of Ben Ravenswood himself, Anna wanted him to be the one trustworthy person among the many who had failed her.

Anna stretched out on the couch with a book she'd been intending to read. Ben would be back, by sunset he'd said. And Theresa would be able to return with the baby tomorrow if Juney felt she was up to it. Until then, Anna held the promise of their return to her quiet, separate life like an approaching holiday. She would enjoy them while they were hers, then learn to live without them later.

BEN KNEW ANNALEE WOULDN'T approve, but he just couldn't help himself. Rather than putting her through the trauma of telling him about her ordeal, he, as a policeman, could do what no ordinary person could do. He could ask to see the case file.

After stopping by his house to get cleaned up and change clothes, Ben had spent two hours on the phone until he'd tracked down the detective assigned to cold cases in Fairfield County, Connecticut. The case of Annalee Winters was colder than most. Almost Ice Age, the detective had quipped. There wasn't much in the file besides her testimony and, stored in the evidence room, the dress she'd been wearing when she escaped.

"Do you have some new evidence or a similar crime that might connect?" the detective had asked.

Not wanting to give away too much because he had basically nothing, Ben had merely replied, "Possibly."

"Well, you're welcome to come up and look at what we've got."

"I just might do that," he'd replied.

Ben hung up the phone no better off than he'd been the day before as far as learning more about Annalee. And he felt guilty on top of that. Annalee seemed to think she had to hide from the world in general rather than just the man who'd abducted her.

Rolling his chair over to his computer, Ben signed on the Internet and searched for kidnapping, Connecticut, Annalee Winters.

What came up made his jaw tight. Story after story about the poor little heir of the Winters Pharmaceutical fortune kidnapped for ransom. In the beginning there were organized searches, sightings in four states and a flurry of false claims and demands. There were stories of the FBI taking over the case and the waiting, waiting, waiting for a bona fide ransom demand. This was followed by accusations that Eugene Winters had refused to pay for his daughter. Winters Pharmaceutical stock fell like a stone.

Into the second month, the stories shifted to the probable tragic fate of Annalee Winters. Cadaver-sniffing dogs had been brought onto the estate and the surrounding area. The more time that passed, the more sure everyone seemed to be that she was dead, and that the perpetrator could be living among them, or be someone closer to Annalee herself. Pictures of Annalee's father hiding his face behind the darkened glass of his limo were what they printed.

Then, four months three days and seven hours after she'd disappeared, the press seemed more shocked than pleased to announce that Annalee had been found. *Found* was not the proper term since she walked herself, barefoot, scratched and undernourished into the police station of a tiny town in Upstate New York. Thankfully there were no pictures of her there. Someone had managed to protect her for a short time.

But later, it seemed as though she'd been followed constantly. As Ben clicked through screens he saw photos of a young and thin Annalee leaving an office building. The caption read Kidnapped Heiress Visits Psychiatrist.

The pictures were old and grainy, but Ben could barely stand to look into those haunted eyes. Oh, Anna.

Stories followed on every movement she made in the next few months. Telephoto shots of her at school, some even in her own backyard. Finally, almost suddenly, the stories stopped. Ben hoped that the press had finally gotten a conscience and stopped hounding a girl who'd already been through hell.

The last story printed was about the firing of a housekeeper who'd taken money to allow photographers access to Annalee. The article stated that the housekeeper planned to sue Mr. Eugene Winters for dismissing her without cause because she hadn't done anything, she'd only taken the money.

Now Ben knew why Anna needed to hide.

The policeman in him wanted to know why the authorities had never come up with a suspect, although he understood the low odds of closing cases involving a random act. If the man had been a total stranger to Anna and her family, as most serial criminals were, then there would be very little for the police to go on. The growing sophistication of criminal profilers and databases in the nineties would have been too late for a fifteen-year-old crime.

He could fly to Connecticut and be back in one day, he figured. But not yet. Right now he had Theresa Smith to deal with—her appearance at her boyfriend's trial would fulfill the bench warrant. He'd make sure she got back to her family, or wherever she wanted to go. Then he'd be free to concentrate on Annalee.

TRANSCRIPTION of taped hypnosis session with female minor X, 14 years old. Excerpted from psychiatric evaluation of Dr. Antony Desillio, Ph.D., State of New York. Also present at session: Detective Albert Jacobson, Connecticut State Police, and Agent Samuel Ettings, FBI.

"Now concentrate…I want you to remember the kidnapper. What he looked like. Anything about his—"

"Don't make me look at the faces!"

(Sob and rustling movement)

"He'll find me!"

"Put your hands down. No one will find you. You're safe now."

(Long silence)

"That's better. Now tell us about the faces. Were these other people you saw?"

"No, they were cats—tigers…with blood—"

(Several gasping breaths)

"With blood coming out of their mouths."

(Rustling movements throughout the room)

"You saw this man kill tigers?"

(Surprised voice of Agent Ettings)

"No, sir. He only made them bleed. He said the tigers would never die and they could always find me. Find me and kill me."

"Tell me about the man's face. What did he look like?"

"He has dark hair and he's taller than me. He smells like cinnamon gum and cigarettes. He—his

hands are soft like a girl's, but really strong. He could hold me down with one hand."

(Deep breath)

"His eyes are blue but sometimes green. He said he could see inside my head. One time he killed a bird he'd brought me from the drugstore, because he said he knew I wanted him to do it. But I didn't. I wanted him to kill me."

"Do you remember anything significant about his voice?"

"I remember he always said no."

CHAPTER NINE

ANNA HAD PUT HER BOOK DOWN and looked out the windows a minimum of twenty times before she finally gave in and moved to the porch to sit with the dogs. From there she could watch the road without feeling silly for acting like a jumping bean.

Sunset.

The leaves on the trees to the west were reflecting gold as the sun sank toward the horizon. She compelled herself to remain still, to listen to the birds calling and the busy rustling of the squirrels in the leaves searching for acorns. This land and cabin comprised her world, her place, and she needed to lose herself in it once more. The nervous flutter of anticipation nagging her was worrisome. Unfamiliar.

Ben.

He'd said he'd be back at sunset.

And she'd allowed herself to count on that. A mistake, she knew, but this time she lacked the will to fight. She'd learned long ago that having anyone in her life, from her father to his employees, her friends to her teachers, was like an open door to her secrets.

Strangers were always probing the locks on her secrets, checking for weakness or carelessness. And money, except in the case of her father, had always been the key. Her father had only thought to help, yet by speaking out, he'd hurt her the most. All of it had gone bad.

And now Ben said he wanted to help. She'd told him her secret, or part of it, and he said he'd be back at sunset.

The crunch of gravel under tires announcing the approach of a truck made Anna's pulse leap and pound in her temples. She took a deep, calming breath to at least appear unaffected. Ben had already gate-crashed into her life, no sense letting him feel at home. Anna knew he couldn't stay.

AS SOON AS BEN'S TRUCK CLEARED the trees along the driveway, he saw Annalee sitting on the porch. *She's waiting for me.* He experienced alternate doses of amazement and hope. It was more welcome than he'd expected. Two weeks ago she'd have faced him with a gun, or simply watched him from the windows.

Warmth expanded his chest. The fact that she'd trusted him with her troubled past and had allowed, if not totally welcomed, him into her present still confounded him. He swore to himself that he wouldn't muck it up.

After coming to a stop, he opened the truck's door and heard Anna talking to the dogs.

"You can let this one sit on the porch," she said, then smiled at him. "At least for now."

Anna's smile nearly stopped Ben in his tracks. He'd seen her controlled wit, her sarcasm meant to create distance, but he'd never witnessed her true and open humor. It scared him a little. Because now that he'd seen it, he didn't ever want to go back to not being included.

"Hey," he said, then made a show of giving the dogs a warning frown as he walked up the stairs. He had the urge to lean down and kiss Anna, as any man coming home might do. But he didn't. *Home. Don't make yourself at home. You haven't been invited.* He briefly touched her shoulder however, before relaxing into the rocker facing hers.

"Did you have a nice day?" Anna asked.

Ben chuckled. He thought of saying, *Yes, dear,* but didn't.

"What's so funny?" she asked, although she didn't seem angry, only curious.

"I was just thinking about the first time I came up here and you threatened to shoot me and feed me to the dogs."

Anna lowered her chin, with a ready-to-fight expression. "That could still be arranged," she threatened. The humor in her eyes took out the sting, and the dogs ignored it altogether.

"I went by to check on Theresa," he informed her. He could see by the interest in her expression that he'd changed to the right subject.

"How is she? How's the baby?"

"Juney says she's doing well. She said to tell you the baby is nursing, although if you want to know more about that, you'll have to ask her."

Anna shrugged. "You probably know as much about babies as I do," she confessed. "As you can see—" she indicated the dogs "—my family circle is rather small."

The words *I've been meaning to talk to you about that* were on the tip of his tongue, but again he kept quiet. He'd already spent half the day digging around in her past and it made him feel as if he'd broken some unspoken promise between them.

"I'll go get her tomorrow," Anna said.

"Are you going to let her stay here then?" Ben asked.

"I guess that depends on you. Are you going to try to take her into custody?"

Ben leaned back in the rocker and crossed one leg, ankle on knee. He'd heard the word *try* and briefly wondered how far Anna would go to protect the girl. "I had to tell the sheriff we'd found her. Otherwise we'd be wasting manpower and time searching. Having a bunch of men crashing around in the woods can get dangerous...to the men.''

Anna almost smiled again and Ben relaxed. As long as she was talking person to person instead of using a gun as an interpreter, he figured things would go all right.

''When and where is this trial?''

''On the eleventh in Atlanta.''

Anna folded her hands and faced him squarely. ''After she testifies, she's free to go, right?''

He nodded.

''That's good,'' Anna said, ''because go, she will. I'll make sure of it.''

The deliberate tone of her voice and the unmoving conviction in her gaze made a believer out of Ben. ''Why did you decide to help her?'' He asked the question he'd been pondering since he'd found the trail Theresa had left to Anna's cabin.

Anna looked out, past his truck, to the trees and the rapidly setting sun and her expression hardened. ''She reminded me of someone I used to know,'' she said, without meeting his gaze.

''Someone you cared about?''

She looked at him then but the distance remained. ''You could say that.''

Ben took a chance. ''Did anyone ever help you, Anna?''

She didn't flinch. ''No.'' Then, subject at an end, she drew herself together and pushed out of her rocker. She stood with one shoulder braced against the porch column and stared down at him. "So, are you going home or are you planning to trespass on my land again? Isn't there someone at home worried about you?"

He worked his mouth into his most charming smile, hoping to cut the distance between them once more. "No, there's nobody waiting for me at home. I thought I'd sleep under the moon one more night before I report back to the real world."

At the mention of the moon, he saw Anna start slightly, as if she'd forgotten running into his arms naked and marked with blood until he'd brought it up.

"You like the moon, do you?" Anna's voice and manner had changed again, challenging, almost seductive. She seemed to be daring him to stand face-to-face with her so-called craziness.

He paid her back in kind by nodding. "Some of the most beautiful things I've ever seen have been in moonlight."

Anna watched him, silently, for so long he thought she might be thinking of ways to dismember him for bullying his way into her life in the first place. But she smiled instead. The sort of smile that could bring tears to a softhearted person. Ben was tougher than that.

"Do you want to eat dinner with me? As a

thank-you for helping Theresa?'' She asked. *Not for being my friend.* The implication was clear.

Ben didn't hesitate. ''Cooking over a fire is great, for a day or two. But chili and beanie weenies get old after that. Right now, your offer stands as the best I've had all day.''

HOURS LATER, lying on his unzipped sleeping bag, arms braced under his head, Ben watched the moon rise above the mountains in the distance and felt a shiver of premonition. For the rest of his days he'd never look at the moon in the same way again, not without remembering Annalee. The implication was sobering because he knew Anna could forget him in an instant. He'd seen her do it, watched her retreat back into her solitary world, leaving him feeling like a howling dog on the wrong side of the fence.

Dinner had been civilized, he supposed, although most of his questions had gone unanswered, diverted to other subjects. He'd learned how her dogs were trained, how many ways there were to cook chicken, and what kind of music went best with certain wines. Nothing about Anna, the long, empty spaces of her life, or how she intended to help Theresa. It seemed that when Anna had given him the most tragic secret of her past, she'd decided to keep the rest of her secrets even further out of reach. As if she was expecting some signal or test before truly trusting him. Or maybe because she'd never truly trust him.

He'd almost brought up his search on the computer and his call to the Connecticut authorities ten different times. But his inner "too little, too late" gauge had strangled the urge. His gut feeling said she was waiting for him to go one step too far, then he'd be shut out forever. He thought of Juney's words about justice. Anna had not received justice, so she would be the judge and jury in the court of her life. Ben had the suspicion not too many men had gotten as close as he had, physically and emotionally, and that he needed to tread carefully for both Anna's sake, and his own.

He gazed at the moon again and listened to the night sounds around him: crickets, cicadas and wind in the trees. No traffic noise here, or booming car radios and blaring TVs. He'd moved back to the mountains to get away from all of that, and to leave the gunfire, the violence that had defined his life in Atlanta.

To get over his guilt about Sharon.

He'd put her death in a deep, silent place inside, but like Anna and her memories, the sight of Sharon covered in blood, dying in a dirty parking lot, would rise to haunt him if he wasn't careful. It stayed in his mind like an extra nerve ending, waiting to be disturbed. He'd always thought he deserved to be haunted because her death was his fault, even though he'd been shot as well.

But after hearing Annalee speak haltingly about her ordeal, he'd felt differently. None of what happened to Anna had been her fault, yet she was even more haunted than Ben. A sad testimony to human minds that managed to lose the good memories when overwhelmed by the bad.

Ben drew in a deep lungful of the night breeze and looked away from the moon. The light followed, however. Even when he closed his eyes, it seemed he could see it through his eyelids like a spotlight. How must Annalee feel when the moon called to her?

The hooting of an owl sounded close and loud, leaves rustled and trees creaked. Ben relaxed and stared at the stars, hoping for peace and a little sleep before dawn. It was the last night he'd spend so close to Annalee, and he could at least hope for a good dream.

He heard her, before he saw her.

She made no effort to be quiet, or to call out to him for that matter. Ben turned to face the sound of her footsteps and saw Anna standing next to the shadowed trunk of a pine tree a dozen feet away. Like an Indian woman, she had a blanket around her shoulders draped over some sort of long gown or dress, and her hair was loose. The moon shadows shifted, making her appearance ghostly and unreliable. She might have been made of moonlight and darkness.

The Crazy Woman of Rain Mountain.

A chill traveled over his skin and the sensation had nothing to do with the weather. Ben wondered if the memories he'd been so recently confronting had come back to bite him. Death and grief and sadness. The male in him remembered Anna on the ridge top, naked. The policeman in him stared at her hands, searching for the knife.

ANNA WASN'T SURE why she'd walked up the hill to Ben. She'd been restless and unable to sleep, nothing unusual about that. The moon had finally drawn her out, although being past full, the power had lessened.

Perhaps it had been Ben himself, and not the moon, who had called to her. He'd been reaching out to her from the first day she'd seen him in town. He'd always greeted her on the street, sometimes ending up in line behind her to buy stamps at the post office, or smiling, holding the door of the grocery store so she could exit with her bags.

In the past two days he'd stumbled into most of her well-guarded secrets and still he remained, waiting for something, waiting for her. Reaching out.

She watched as he pushed up on one elbow, his features obscured by the shadows of the trees.

"Are you okay?" he asked. His voice sounded a little harsh, official, and it surprised her. Not the voice of the friendly man she'd had dinner with earlier. She wasn't sure whether to move forward or go back to the cabin.

"Yes," she answered, and remained where she was.

"Out walking in the moonlight?"

Anna gazed up through the trees at the innocent moon. The moon made her invisible, or as close to it as she would ever be. She knew what Ben was really asking, however. "Walking, yes. Not like last night." She held up her empty hands. "No blood."

A heartbeat of silence passed, then his voice seemed more normal. "Can't say I'm sorry to hear that."

Anna took a few steps toward him so she could see his expression in the dark. She'd missed his crooked smile and the mischief in his eyes. She'd never missed anyone else, except her mother. The bad man had loomed too large in her nightmares. She couldn't afford to miss anyone, she had to hide, to run away.

Run away, run away.

"Were you asleep?" she asked but already knew the answer. She had to buy time until she figured out why she'd been drawn to him.

"No. I was listening to the crickets and thinking—'' he hesitated ''—how much I'm going to miss this place.''

Surprised again, she stared, wanting to see his eyes but unable to; they were only a glimmer in the dark. An appropriate reply seemed impossible, her mind had drifted past appropriate when the moon had risen.

Ben sat up and arranged the edges of the sleeping bag next to him. ''Care to sit down and listen to the crickets together?'' A low chuckle followed. ''I don't know what kind of wine goes best with cricket song, but I'm willing to discuss the possibilities.''

Anna felt herself smile and a clenched part of her relaxed. This man never ceased to amaze her, and it seemed as though she hadn't been able to shock him in the least. Or, if she did, he'd covered it well. She nodded, then crossed the distance between them and took a seat in the shadows on the edge of his sleeping bag. With her back to him, she faced the moon.

Ben straightened beside her, propped on one elbow. ''What can I do for you, Annalee?'' he said with an ache in his voice she'd never heard before. ''Do you want to talk?''

She turned to look at him. ''I don't know,'' she answered honestly.

He slowly raised one hand and pushed a few strands of hair out of her face then cupped her chin in his palm. The touch was so gentle, Anna felt tears rise in her eyes. He ran a callused thumb along her cheekbone like a blind man mapping her face. Anna turned into his touch. His palm smelled of pine sap and something indefinably male.

"Will you stay here with me and watch the moon?"

That's what she'd wanted all along. And it took Ben to figure it out. She'd wanted to share the moon with him, so that he could feel its pull yet keep her from following too far. She nodded.

Ben moved over and patted the spot near his hip. "Stretch out, we'll watch it together."

And to her own amazement, she did.

It took thirty minutes for the moon's light to find them on the sleeping bag under the pines. One moment, they'd been in companionable silence in the shadows, Anna feeling Ben's presence next to her like the fulfillment of a wistful dream, the next they were illuminated by the bright, blue-white light of midnight.

The wildness uncoiled in Anna as she finally realized what she wanted from Ben.

BEN FELT Anna stir and experienced a stab of disappointment. She was leaving. He'd hoped, when she realized he wouldn't hurt her, that she'd relax. He fought the urge to hold her arm or her hand, anything to keep her next to him. He sat up as she did.

"You don't have to go," he said, losing the battle with stoic silence.

She looked at him as the moon turned her hair to silver and smiled. "Shh," she said, and put one hand flat on his chest to nudge him back down. With two quick motions, she removed her boots, then she rose to her knees over him.

Ben's heart pounded under the influence of adrenaline mixed with anticipation. As he watched Anna slide the blanket off her shoulders he decided that even if she killed him there in the moonlight, he had to see what she would do next.

Wearing some kind of sleeveless dress, Anna's bare arms were painted by moonlight. She raised them and pushed her hair off her shoulders as she turned her face to the moon. He'd seen sun worshipers do the same, but there was no warmth in the moonlight, only cool mystery and silver visions.

She smiled, lowered her arms and grasped the bottom of her dress. Without pausing, she drew the dress over her head:

Naked.

Ben had long since lost the ability to talk or even beg. The ache to touch her, to do everything from make love to her to shield her from the world, paralyzed him. He'd lie there until the sun came up if that's what it took. He had to wait for Anna.

She leaned over him to brush a hand along his face not unlike the way he'd touched her earlier. The contact made him suck in a quick breath and his hands rose in response.

"Be still," she whispered, and waited for him to lie flat again.

He could barely speak. "Tell me what you want me to do," he said, the choked feeling in his throat making his voice sound harsh.

"Be still and I'll show you."

Sighing, he gave in. As usual, under Anna's influence, he would stand back and wait. But in this case, parts of his body were arguing over whose vote had put his brain in charge.

With the deliberation of a child, Anna began unbuttoning his shirt. She made no move to touch his skin, or indicate her intentions as she pushed the shirt open off his shoulders. Willingly under her spell, Ben raised up slightly and helped her free his arms from the sleeves. This time when she put her hand on his chest to push him down, however, the cool touch of her palm caused his heart to beat even faster, sending a new rush of blood to his groin.

Her fingers went to his belt and after a few swift moves she was pushing his loose hunting pants downward. He stopped her at his hips. He had no

idea if she knew where she was going but felt the
need to curb the speed a little.

"I want them off," she said, facing him as
though he couldn't possibly have an objection to
being as naked as she was.

Ben stared into her moon-dazzled eyes for several seconds, searching for the right thing to say.

"Oh, hell," he finally muttered. Fool or not,
there was no way he could walk away from her,
not now. Without waiting for her help, he sat up
and reached for his boot laces. Anna leaned back
on her haunches like a patient wood nymph as he
removed his boots then kicked off his pants. He
left his briefs, just in case.

"Lie down," she said when he'd finished.

He did. The moonlight played over both of them
now and Ben felt its attraction. The woods around
them were light and dark, no middle tones. If life
was more like that, everyone could live it better.

As he stared at Anna, waiting for her to decide,
she smiled and leaned over him. She took each of
his arms and placed first his right, then his left over
his head. He tried to catch her wrists but she pulled
away, patting his hands back into position. In one
lithe movement she stood and straddled him, sitting on his belly.

Ben wanted to pray but it didn't seem appropriate. Anna had thrown her head back and appeared
to be conversing with the moon again. With her

weight on him and the touch of her naked thighs against his waist and sides, he wouldn't do anything to stop this. Not even if she...

Anna suddenly leaned over him again, her long, dark hair tumbling forward, nearly obscuring her face. She ran her hands along his arms until her hands circled his wrists, then she lowered her face to his, but stopped before actually touching. The smell of her hair falling around him reminded Ben of waterfalls and white pines. He wanted to kiss her and made the effort.

She pulled back slightly. "Be still." Her words were a whisper against his lips.

Frustrated but unwilling to spoil her plan, he stayed still. She looked at him then. He knew the golden color of her eyes, the light in them when she smiled, the darkness when she withdrew. But in the silver and shadows of the moonlight, everything seemed strange.

"You don't have to worry. You're with me now and I won't let anyone hurt you," she said.

Ben's lust versus sanity meter took a dip. What if she really was crazy? That would mean he was taking unfair advantage. His line of thought nearly made him groan. A beautiful, naked woman had him pinned down and he was worried he might be doing the wrong thing. Jeez. What an ass. He heroically tried to bring things back to normal.

"Annalee? What can I do for you?"

She smiled again, not at all perturbed. "We want to touch you?"

Ben almost squirmed. "Who's we?"

"The moon and I. See?" She ran her fingers lightly over his face then down across his chest, watching her own shadow. "It won't hurt."

She seemed to be waiting for permission so Ben nodded. He had to see it through. To see what the Witch of Rain Mountain had in mind. Crazy or sane.

ANNA GAZED DOWN AT BEN and felt an exhilarating sense of power. Maybe it was the moon, or being in control, or simply her wanting of Ben, but Anna didn't intend to stop. For so long she'd remembered being the powerless victim, now she would be the predator.

And Ben wasn't afraid.

Something about his surrender made her want to pull up. She knew she was acting a little crazy, or maybe a lot crazy, but she'd had no experience with normal so she would have to use what she knew.

Holding his wrists, she smelled his hair, then it tangled with hers, then his ears, his neck, his mouth. His lips twitched…so close to hers. No kissing, yet. He shifted restlessly when she rubbed her face against the smooth skin of his chest with its dusting of hair. She heard him groan. Harboring a secret smile, she pushed off him and sat close to his side.

In the moonlight his long limbs looked hard, like the marble of a statue except for the slight furring of hair covering his legs. He was beautiful. How could she have ever been afraid of Ben? She moved one hand and placed it over the bright whiteness of his underwear, over the obvious bulge of his erection.

With a shocked intake of breath, Ben halfway sat up, and Anna wanted to laugh at her own aggression. Laughter didn't seem appropriate, however, and since she'd already been labeled as crazy there was no use proving the point. She moved her hand slowly over the length of him and, when his hips rose to push against her fingers, Anna totally forgot about laughter. His reaction sent a slow-moving flow of warmth from her thighs to her womb.

She hadn't expected that. She knew what was hidden beneath her hand, how it looked and its purpose. But she'd never experienced the echoing ache inside her own body, the wanting of something she'd only read about in books.

"Annalee?" Ben's breathless voice was calling her back.

She moved her attention from his groin to his face. As she watched, he touched her arm with his fingers and tugged her toward him.

''Please come here.''

She hesitated for a moment yet he didn't press. Then to please herself, she straddled him again before stretching out full-length on top of him. With her ear against his chest, she heard his breath rushing in and out of his lungs. The palm of his hand moved along her spine, caressing, calming. It was the most perfect moment she could ever remember experiencing. Anna's eyes unexpectedly filled with tears. She'd never dreamed she could get so physically close to a man. Not after the bad man, even though he hadn't done all he could have to her. Now, for the first time she knew why women, normal women anyway, wanted to fall in love, to find a partner, a lover.

For the touching, for the ache of welcome inside.

Ben must have felt her changing emotions because he lifted her chin so he could look into her face. She couldn't speak but she remembered he'd wanted a kiss. She only had to think it for Ben to make it real.

BEN DECIDED THAT he was the one losing his mind. His body had already been lost, to Anna. The feel of her bare breasts against his chest, and the flutter of her heart beating next to his made him weak at the knees. He wanted her more than he'd ever wanted a woman, and that was hard to admit. The other hard-to-admit part was no matter how odd Anna acted, he still wanted her. If she asked him to get on all fours and howl at the moon, he likely would do it, for a kiss.

Her soft mouth, the one he'd watched as they'd talked, as they'd had dinner, as they'd said good-bye, opened against his in complete surrender. She seemed willing, after torturing him for her amusement, to let him take the lead. He had to concentrate in order not to scare her. Slowly he tasted her with his tongue and after a slight jump of shock she relaxed.

He wondered who the last man in her life had been and felt an unreasonable stab of anger toward him. The man who should have held on to the Witch of Rain Mountain, who should have protected her from her demons, from the world, from the moon.

He kissed her deeper then, to make up for the hundreds of times he'd wanted to in the past. And to wipe out any old, lingering memories. Anna kissed him back, lunge for lunge, tongue for tongue. They didn't part until they ran out of air.

"I want to be inside you," Ben confessed as he pushed his face into her hair.

"Yes."

Ben wasn't sure what he'd expected her to say, but yes wasn't the first guess. He bracketed her shoulders and made her look into his eyes. "Yes, what?"

"I want that, too." She seemed perfectly sane, perfectly in control and, judging by the soft set of her mouth and the pulse pounding under his fingers, perfectly ready to continue where they'd left off.

"Are you sure?" He couldn't help it, he had a sister after all.

She nodded and moved in for another kiss.

Slow down, Ben's brain ordered. And he tried, he really did. But kissing Anna was like having Thanksgiving dinner in front of you and your favorite dessert waiting in the kitchen. A feast. They were both breathless when he shifted her weight to bring them side by side, a position that would enable him to use his hands and his mouth to savor the rest of her body. He watched Anna's features as he settled her on her back, then leaned over her as she gazed up at the moon.

"No!" She pushed at his chest until he backed away. A moment later she was sitting up.

She ducked her head away from the light. "I can't look at the moon when you…" She didn't sound crazy, she sounded heartbroken.

Making an attempt to pull himself together, Ben gave in. "We don't have to—"

"He made me look at the moon when he touched me," she confessed. She gazed at Ben, her eyes dark and unfathomable. "I need to see your face in the light, to remember it's you."

Ben watched Anna's fractured expression in the moonlight and experienced a white-hot will to commit murder. Not a good thing for a police officer. If he'd known the identity of the man who'd hurt Anna, he'd be the one on his way to prison.

Her hand found his chest again, pushing him onto his back. "Lie down."

He covered her hand with his own. "You don't have to do anything you don't want to do."

"I want to," she said, her voice stronger than before. "With you. I do."

TRANSCRIPTION of taped session with female minor X, 14 years old. Excerpted from psychiatric evaluation of Dr. Antony Desillio, Ph.D., State of New York. Interview by Dr. Grace Portman, specialist in molestation cases.

"I'd like for you to draw a picture of yourself, then one of the man who abducted you. Will you try that?"

"What do you want to see? His face?"

"I want to see whatever you remember, everything."

(Patient willingly draws for thirty minutes)

"This is me."

"Black and white. Why didn't you use any of the colors?"

"This is what I remember."

"So, this is you, wearing a gray dress hiding in the corner. Are you hiding from the man?"

"No."

"Not from the man. From what then?"

(Patient points to a window in the drawing and a round object)

"I'm hiding from the moon. That's when he makes me look at the tigers."

"May I see the picture of him?"

(Long silence)

"You've used color and...quite a lot of detail. Did the man always visit you without wearing clothes?"

"Only on the nights of the full moon."

"Speaking for the record, the drawing is very anatomically correct."

(To patient)

"What is the red on his arms and his hands?"

"Blood from the tigers."

(Pause. Shuffling of papers)

"You've done well on the drawings. Let's go on. I'd like you to take this doll and show me any place the man touched you."

(Patient refuses to accept doll)

"He touched me everywhere, some places more than others, he used to give me baths, wash my hair, but on the full moon he would do the bad things."

"What bad things?"

"Things I didn't want him to do—no matter what. But he did them anyway."

Notes: *Patient has been examined by a forensic gynecologist and technically, according to the report, she was not raped, although the damage to her psyche is as great or greater than if the actual act had been committed. I attribute this to the cumulative effect of being held and repeatedly threatened for the four months of her captivity. I suspect it will take years of therapy for her to make any progress toward normalcy.*

CHAPTER TEN

ANNA WASN'T SURE what she'd expected, but being with Ben was more intoxicating, more pleasurable, than anything she'd read in her books. Everything about him seemed to resonate inside her. Male versus female: the way he smelled, the feel of his warm, rough hands on her smoother, cooler skin, the sounds he made when she knew she had excited him, the way he sank into her body and captured her inside and out.

"Do whatever you want," he'd said, and she'd taken him at his word. He'd only interrupted long enough to explore her breasts with his hands and his mouth, and to rock her against the hardest part of him until she thought she might burst into flames.

Only you can prevent forest fires.

Forget being safe, she wanted more.

Anna slid off Ben long enough to tug his briefs down. Helpful, as always, he kicked them off. Then she was astride him again, giving herself no chance to cool down or calm down. She wanted the entire experience, had a willing partner who made her tremble with every touch. Nothing could change her mind. Not the past, not the future, not even the moon.

Renewing the rocking motion that had created such titillating friction before now took Anna's breath away. The hot, smooth length of him rubbing against the most sensitive part of her body, without any barriers, made her shiver with pleasure.

Ben pulled her down for a kiss then held her close. "Are you ready?" His voice was hoarse. "I don't think I can stand this much longer. It's making me—"

Anna's mind was on the delicious feel of him, and the way her body quaked for more. More of what Ben could give her. "Yes, I—"

He shifted his hips at the sound of yes, and Anna arched away from his chest to take him inside. She felt him enter partway then stop. He seemed to freeze.

"Anna?" Her name sounded ragged in the chorus of night sounds.

She hadn't known whether or not he would be able to tell. Obviously he could. Before he could say anything to derail her intent, she forced her hips downward. Pushing until, after a momentary pain, she felt completely filled and knew she was no longer a virgin.

Ben's arms clamped around her and dragged her

to his chest, holding them both motionless except for his panting breath and her pounding heart. She could still feel him inside her. *Please don't be angry. You said I could have what I wanted. This is what I wanted.*

"Why didn't you tell me?" he said into her hair. His arms were so tight around her she couldn't have answered if she'd wanted to.

When she didn't answer, he tentatively moved his hips, causing a ripple of renewed heat inside her. "Are you in pain?"

"No," she choked out.

"Do you want to stop?"

"No—please." Anna rocked against him, needing anything, everything. She'd gotten part of what she'd wanted. Now she wanted the rest. A moan rose inside her. "Please don't stop, Ben."

Saying his name must have convinced him. He raised his head and kissed her so sweetly she almost forgot that she held him inside her. Then he put his warm hands on her bottom and showed her a slow, rocking rhythm that made both of them groan in pleasure. Somehow, even though Anna remained on top, she'd lost control. Ben was using his strength and his knowledge of her body to give them both pleasure.

It felt wonderful. It felt magical. It felt…right.

Anna hadn't known it could be like this. She would have smiled at the moon if she'd cared to.

But the moon didn't matter with Ben inside her, making her feel as if she'd been asleep her whole life until now.

"Ah—Anna," Ben growled as he increased the rhythm, caught up in his own pleasure. The sound of his voice, low and urgent, combined with the building heat inside her, sent her over the edge. The word *orgasm* as defined in a medical text had no relation to what Anna experienced. She heard the echo of her own cry in the trees before she collapsed on Ben's chest. It was the most breathtakingly intense pleasure she'd ever known. And the most intimately fulfilling.

Let the moon know, let the bad man know, let everyone know that she was now a woman. She could never be the bad man's little girl again.

Because of Ben.

Anna rested, her face pressed to his chest, feeling the labored rhythm of his lungs as he caught his breath. Ben. How could he ever understand what he'd done for her?

A VIRGIN? WHAT HAD HE DONE?

He had no excuses, he could have stopped. He just hadn't wanted to stop. Hadn't been able to. And Anna had said...oh hell, it didn't really matter what Anna had said. He knew better. How in the world had she made it this far in life without having a lover? Or a husband...someone?

The answer was obvious. He'd read the newspaper reports. She'd been trapped by her notoriety. She'd never had a boyfriend or a fiancé. She'd been held hostage as surely as if she'd never gotten away from the kidnapper. Again anger shivered through him causing Anna to react.

He gently guided her off him and then pulled her close to his side. He nudged her chin up so he could see her face in the moonlight. "Why didn't you tell me?"

She rested one palm against his chest, looking relaxed and unafraid. "Would it have changed anything?"

"Probably," he said, telling the truth.

"Then, that's why," she said, and smiled.

Ben hadn't expected the smile. It threw his conscience for a loop. "You look like the cat that ate the canary," he teased. "Quite satisfied with herself."

"No, I look like a woman who lost her virginity at twenty-nine. I would say it's about time."

About time. Ben wished he could start the evening all over again. He might not be a smooth ladies' man but he could certainly have made the evening more romantic than a tumble in the woods on a ten-year-old sleeping bag. They could've stayed in the cabin after dinner. There would have been clean sheets and candlelight, time to tease and appreciate.

No moon.

"I would have done things differently if I'd known."

Anna actually chuckled at that. "You put me in charge, remember?" Then she went serious on him. "What you did for me tonight was amazing, Ben Ravenswood. I won't ever forget it."

Ben wanted to get lost in the rich, emotional tone of her voice, but unfortunately, her words sounded suspiciously like goodbye. He wasn't ready to discuss the future, except for one issue. "You know we didn't use any protection when we…"

She watched him in silence.

"There's always the possibility you could end up like Theresa, with a baby." He had to swallow before he could say the words because the image exposed a longing he hadn't expected. "My baby."

The hand on his chest contracted briefly, but it was the only sign of reaction on her part. "I know where babies come from, Deputy. I'll worry about that if the problem arises."

Ben would have paid more attention to the fact that, for once in his experience, Anna didn't have a plan and a backup plan for every type of problem. What threw him off was the fact she'd called him "deputy."

She stirred next to him then sat up. He knew she

was about to leave. He felt the pain of her being done with him and anger that, after they'd just shared the most intimate of acts, she'd go back to her old defensiveness. What had happened to the trust? He remained still. He needed to say it all or nothing, and right then he couldn't trust himself not to scare her.

She dressed in silence, picked up her blanket and stood. Then she left, although she stopped at the trees to look back at him. In darkness again since the moon had passed, Ben made no move to cover his nakedness. If she could walk away as if they were strangers, he at least had nothing to be ashamed about.

"Good night," she said, before disappearing into the trees like a ghost.

WHEN JUNEY BRIDGER OPENED the door the next morning, she stared at Anna for several seconds before saying anything. Then she smiled.

"Good morning. Come in."

Entering Juney's house was like stepping from the calm into the storm. Compared to the quiet urgency Anna had witnessed the night Theresa's baby had been born, today the house had a raucous, circuslike atmosphere, filled as it was with children, laughter, and five different conversations going at once.

The adults in the room, three women along with

Theresa, quieted slightly to stare at the newcomer, but the children continued their games undeterred by the arrival of a new adult.

"These are my daughters," Juney said. "You met Sarah the other night." The daughter in question waved. "The other two are Rae and Jane." Juney raised a hand toward the six children of different ages playing on the floor and one in a crib near the wall. "These are my grandbabies. As you can see, even without anyone from the outside, we stay busy with midwifery. I won't go into which ones belong to who—we love them all the same."

Looking down at the children, who were totally involved in their own small world, made something in Anna's chest hurt. Something about being protected, being loved. The way the world should be, but for some never would be. Suddenly Juney touched her arm and Anna felt jolted back to the present—the dark past receding like an echo of imagined pain.

"Come and see our newest addition," Juney said, a shade of sympathy in her voice.

Anna stared at the midwife, unable to fathom how the woman knew the things she knew. It was as though they were having a silent conversation about the past, the future, the pain and the fear. Not knowing how to ask, she kept the questions to herself and allowed Juney to guide her to Theresa.

Theresa was sitting in the same rocker she'd occupied the first night they'd come to the cabin. But this time she wasn't sick or afraid. As the girl gazed up at Anna, she smiled and the wistful feeling of loss that had gripped Anna earlier eased. The runaway with the dirty face and tangled hair was gone. Theresa looked more like an eighteen-year-old girl should look: smiling, untroubled and hopeful.

Theresa held up her daughter. "Here she is," the proud mother said. "Juney said she's already gained a few ounces."

Without moving, Anna studied the pink-faced baby wrapped in the lightweight blanket. The baby's eyes were closed but her little mouth was puckered up, a bubble of saliva suspended between her lips.

"She looks perfect," Anna said, unable to think of anything more appropriate.

"You want to hold her?" Theresa asked. Then she glanced at the closest of Juney's daughters. "She's been passed around so much since she was born, I'm surprised she knows which one of us is her mother."

The other women laughed. "Babies know, believe me," Sarah said. "Come dinnertime, nobody else will do."

"Here, take her," Theresa said to Anna. "I just fed her so she'll probably sleep."

Without Anna's conscious consent, Juney took

the baby from Theresa and settled her into Anna's arms. "If you're going to be the baby's godmother, you need to get acquainted."

Startled, Anna faced the midwife. "Her godmother?"

Juney smiled unconcerned and waited for Theresa to say something.

"I, um." For the first time, Theresa looked like the nervous runaway who'd shown up on Anna's doorstep. "I thought...since you helped us so much. I wanted—" After one long, loving gaze at her daughter, Theresa finished, "I named her Annabelle, after you, sort of. I wasn't sure you'd want her to be Annalee."

Juney brought a straight-backed chair for Anna, and her weakened knees gladly accepted the invitation to sit.

"I think Annabelle is a beautiful name," Juney said, and each of her daughters added their agreement.

All that remained was for Anna to speak. But her throat felt welded shut. A thousand reasons went through her mind about why having an innocent baby named after her could be a huge mistake. These women were acting as if they had no idea she was cursed. That she was called crazy, a witch. Not to mention the way her life had been destroyed. A baby with her name would be given the worst kind of legacy.

Juney touched her shoulder. "She gets to start brand-new, and you've been a part of that. I'm sure she'll be honored to have your name."

Anna forced her attention to Theresa. The girl looked ready to cry. *Brand-new. She gets to start brand-new.* Anna plastered a smile on her face and gazed down at the tiny girl who'd made an entrance into a world no one had planned for her. "You get to choose later. Right now I think I'll call you Belle so we don't get confused."

Everyone in the room seemed to relax, especially Theresa. Anna sat with the warm, heavier-than-she-looked weight of her goddaughter in her arms and felt as though she'd been dragged into another dimension. A dimension where inhabitants remained the same but the entire world around them changed. In the past week, after years of keeping her life simple and safe, Anna had taken in a stranger, become a godmother...had found a lover.

Ben. Thinking of Ben made her heart hurt. She knew she'd done everything wrong, blindsided by the depths of her neediness. All this time she thought she could do without anyone in her life. And she could. What she hadn't calculated was how much she might want someone in her life.

Anna put her pinky in one of Belle's tiny hands and the baby tightened her fingers around it. Unconditional love, a feeling so far out of Anna's experience she couldn't conceive of anything so innocent.

That's what had spooked her the night before. When Ben had been so kind to her, when he'd warned her she could be pregnant with his baby. The place inside her where that kind of love could grow had been ripped out long ago. She might want Ben. But she couldn't love Ben, or his baby. She didn't deserve them and they certainly didn't deserve what was left of her.

Now with little Annabelle in her arms, the best thing Anna could do would be to find her goddaughter and Theresa a new life, a better place to hide than Anna had found for herself. Then she would consider where she would move next—what mountain, what island. The Crazy Woman of Rain Mountain would have to go.

BEN SPENT THE DAY doing paperwork, trying to keep his mind off Annalee, off the moon. He had so many different lines of thought going through his head it was a wonder he could concentrate at all.

He'd left Anna's property with the rising sun illuminating his footsteps, but his mind remained in the dark. What had happened? What the hell had happened? He alternated between feeling like a pervert for touching her to feeling as though she'd used him then walked away. Turning it over and over in his mind hadn't changed a damn thing.

A virgin. How could she have still been a virgin? How could she have allowed him to violate that?

He'd wanted her, there had been no doubt about it. He'd wanted her since the first time he'd seen her stride down the sidewalk in Dalton Falls, silently daring anyone to stand in her way. And, like a winner of the cosmic lottery, he'd gotten what he wanted. Anna naked and willing. Except now he wanted more.

What did you expect, old son? his mind whispered. *True love?*

Not love. He didn't think he had any left after all this time. After Sharon. His time with Sharon felt like a lifetime ago. She and Annalee were so different...he hadn't had time for expectations. Even if he had, he couldn't have expected Anna to call him "deputy" afterward and walk away. Nothing would have prepared him for that.

He didn't know what to make of her reaction, especially since the change followed him mentioning the possibility he'd made her pregnant. She hadn't given him the chance to say he'd take responsibility. After all the pure heat between them, she hadn't even kissed him goodbye.

Typical. He felt like smacking himself in the head. Every time he thought he understood a part of Annalee Evans, she changed into someone else: woman, child, witch or victim. The Crazy Woman of Rain Mountain was driving him crazy. A short trip, some might say.

Ben signed his name to the personal leave form in front of him and pushed it aside. He needed to drive down to Atlanta and see some old friends. Some of them must have a buddy or two in Connecticut. He'd promised himself he'd try to help Annalee before he'd ever touched her. Now since he'd done much more than that, he intended to step into Annalee's past to see what he could find. In order to have any chance in hell to succeed, he needed a cop who would do a favor for another cop.

IT HAD TAKEN ANNA most of the morning to gather up Theresa and the baby, along with the many things Juney was positive they'd need at the cabin, and then get them back to the west side of Rain Mountain. Juney had insisted on feeding them lunch before they left and had personally loaded the rocker Theresa had been using into Anna's four-wheel drive. It was obviously a family heirloom, but Juney wouldn't take no for an answer. Anna had offered to pay her. Juney had shaken her head and told her to bring the rocker back when she had no use for it.

In the end, Juney had accepted only the standard

fee for delivering a baby and when Anna had tried to explain how much she'd helped them, Juney had put an arm around her and squeezed her briefly.

"I had to show you that you aren't alone anymore," she said.

When Anna had started to deny it, Juney said, "You'll see. You'll see."

A FEW HOURS LATER, as the afternoon moved along toward sunset, Anna watched Theresa rock Belle after breast-feeding her and understood the importance of the rocker. Continuity. Although Belle had been moved and jostled—not to mention been sniffed by the dogs—the tiny bundle was totally lacking in fear, which amazed Anna. She, herself, suspected she'd never slept that soundly in her life.

The noise of an approaching car brought Annalee and the dogs to the front windows of the cabin. Against her determined will, Anna's heart pounded hard at her ribs.

Ben.

She felt a tingling anticipation mixed with embarrassment. What would she say to him? How should she act? In seconds her skin went warm from her toes to the roots of her hair. The things she'd let him do to her. The things she'd done to him...

Then the sheriff's department car rolled into

view and Anna's anticipation cooled. She struggled with her disappointment.

Not Ben.

What had she expected, anyway? Ben didn't belong to her. She'd walked away, gone back to her darkness alone.

With practiced moves she went to the door, picked up her shotgun and let the dogs out to greet the visitor before stepping onto the porch. The gun felt so different than the squirming weight of a baby. The comparison was too obvious to overlook, life and death, beginnings and endings. Anna had to harden herself to get back the woman who depended on threat for safety. Juney was wrong—she remained alone.

A man she didn't know rolled down the window. "Ma'am? My name is Rudy Wilkins, Deputy Wilkins." He touched his hat then looked at the dogs before speaking again. "The sheriff wants one of us to come by once in a while and check on Theresa Smith. To make sure she's okay. But Ben Ravenswood told me not to get out of the car."

By that time, Theresa was standing behind her. She hadn't completely recovered from the birth, but she'd put Belle down and looked ready to face anyone. "They're afraid I'll run again," she said in a low voice. "Like having a baby wouldn't slow me down at all.

"I'm still here," she called to the man. "Not goin' anywhere."

"All right, I'll tell the sheriff," he said. "You need anything, call 911."

Anna watched as, with a wave, he started to back up. "Where's Deputy Ben?" she shouted before her usual good sense could stop her.

The deputy halted the car and shrugged. "Went down to Atlanta, that's where he's from. Don't know when he'll be back."

Anna couldn't speak so she waved, as he had a moment before, then watched him turn his car and disappear up the driveway. Her friendly gesture seemed to worry him more than the gun in her arms.

Witch.

Later, over dinner, Theresa brought it up.

"Are you and Deputy Ben...friends?" she asked.

Anna put down the dinner roll she'd been buttering and wiped her fingers on her napkin. In the old days she'd deflected questions with silence or by walking away, but she couldn't walk away from her own dinner table and from Theresa, who already knew too much.

"Well, I don't know for sure. I thought we were but then something happened and now...I don't know."

"Did you have a fight?" Theresa asked, before biting into an ear of buttered corn.

Worse than that, we made love. "No, not a fight."

"Was it the other night when Belle came? The two of you came in half-dressed and you had blood on you. Did he hurt you?"

Anna braced her arms on the table and held Theresa's gaze until the girl put down the corn and wiped her mouth on her napkin.

"I'm sorry. It's none of my business. Please don't change your mind about helping Belle and me."

She seemed so cowed that Anna felt lower than the braided rug on the floor beneath her feet. "Theresa—" for emphasis she reached over and took the girl's hand in hers "—first of all, I gave my word to help you and Belle have a new life and nothing you can do, short of running away, will change that. Secondly, the craziness the other night was mine, the blood was mine and Ben had nothing to do with it other than loaning me his shirt.

"As for what happened between him and me, I'm sure it was my fault." She pulled her hand away and tried to smile like she didn't care.

"Do you love him?" Theresa almost whispered.

Anna sighed and told the truth. "Before you came here I had no idea what true love meant. But now, when I watch you look at Belle, I see it in your eyes. I can see it, but I don't know how to feel it.''

"He looks at you like that. When you're not watching," Theresa said.

Now that she knew what lust was, she answered with a knowing smile. "When he looks at me, he has something else entirely in mind."

"I'm not so sure," the eighteen-year-old going on thirty said. "Jimmy never looked at me like that."

Not wanting to get in any further over her head, Anna prudently changed course. "Speaking of Jimmy, we need to start narrowing down your choices. I have a video about each of the fifty states. I use them when I need to move on. Look through the box and pick out some to watch. It'll help you know what to expect from a new place. Keep in mind you have to go someplace without friends or family. Then after you have some candidates for your next home, we'll go online and send for more information."

"You're pretty good at this, huh?"

"Better than I ever wanted to be. Trust me. If you want to disappear, I'm the right woman to make it happen."

"SHE JUST DISAPPEARED after her father died," the policeman said. "We had little evidence, no suspect and no victim.'' He smiled. ''The press had to start interviewing each other.''

Ben knew he was skirting the line of ethics, but he couldn't help it. Sometimes the rules had to be bent a little. He'd flown to Connecticut on the recommendation of his former captain in Atlanta. Ben couldn't go so far as to reopen the case, but he could dig around a bit.

''So you were on the case?'' he asked the man.

''It was my second year on the force. I tell you, we had every available man assigned to look for that young girl. Most of us had kids of our own and a case like that can be hard to take.''

''I can imagine,'' Ben concurred. ''We just went through something like that down in Georgia— Dalton County.'' He was thinking of the search for Theresa, which wasn't like Anna's case in the least except the trail had led to her cabin. Anna had been forcibly taken and then escaped. What kind of trail had she left behind when she'd been running?

''We never found the Winters girl though.'' The officer shook his head. ''She got away on her own. A religious man would have said it was a miracle. Most of us regular police officers were happy not to find a body. Do you believe the two cases are related? After all this time?''

''Could be. The girl we were looking for showed up on her own too.'' That was as close to a lie as Ben was willing to go. The only way the two cases

were related was due to his using one to get a look
into the other.

The officer shook his head. "Well—" he stood
up "—if you want the medical records and tran-
scripts from the psychiatric profile, you'll have to
go through a judge. They're sealed because she
was a minor at the time. But I can take you down
to the evidence room and show you what we've
got for physical evidence."

Ben followed the officer through the Fairfield,
Connecticut police headquarters into an elevator
and to a desk in the basement. A few moments
later a taped cardboard box with a pair of rubber
gloves on top was placed in his hands.

"This is it," the officer said. "You can sit at
the table over there and look through it. Give it to
Lee here when you're done. I'll be upstairs."

Ben nodded. He took the box to the table and
took his time pulling on the rubber gloves. He
didn't know what he'd find inside this dismal time
capsule from Anna's dark past, but he knew he
wanted to be alone when he found out.

The tape was old and brittle, the box a little
dusty. With the top open though, the contents were
in good shape. A handful of papers documenting
the chain of evidence covered several sealed plastic
bags. One held two cheap plastic hair barrettes too
childish looking for a fourteen-year-old to choose.
As he held the bag up to the light he could see

several strands of long, dark hair still caught in the teeth.

Anna's hair. He remembered Anna saying that the kidnapper had loved to brush her hair. The vicious bolt of anger following the realization that the man who hurt Anna had held these very barrettes in his hands made Ben grit his teeth. As if he'd touched something foul, he set the bag aside and reached for the larger bag beneath it. This one looked like it held clothing.

Ben pulled the package free and turned it over. The material was darkened, stained. Without pausing to guess, he opened the plastic bag and gingerly took out the evidence. He saw lace around the collar of a young girl's dress. It was difficult to imagine the formidable Annalee Evans ever being this young and vulnerable. Lace, for God's sake. As he unfolded the fragile fabric and got a better idea of its shape, Ben felt as if he'd been kicked in the chest.

The dress was dirty, and torn, and stained with blood.

Oh, Anna…

TRANSCRIPTION of taped session with female minor X, 14 years old. Excerpted from psychiatric evaluation of Dr. Antony Desillio, Ph.D., State of New York. Interview by Dr. Grace Portman, specialist in molestation cases.

"Tell me about the blood on the dress you were wearing?"

"It's his blood. He made me wear it."

"You mean the dress?"

(Sound of exasperation)

"No, I told you, he made me wear his blood, always. He said it marked me as his girl. He said I could never get away because his blood wouldn't let me go. The tigers would find me."

"Are those the bloody tigers you described before?"

(Subject nodded)

"But you did get away."

(Another nod)

"But the tigers are still out there."

Notes: Subject shows a high level of posttraumatic stress and classic signs of thought manipulation. At this point in treatment it is difficult to determine what percentage of her memories are true and what percentage hallucination. Recommend a longer course of therapy along with antianxiety drugs. Have discussed committal with parent and will consider as a later course of action if confusion and delusions persist.

CHAPTER ELEVEN

"ANNA?" THERESA CALLED from the bedroom she and Belle shared.

Anna pushed print on her computer and left it to finish the last set of instructions she needed. In the past three days, she and Theresa had narrowed her relocation choices to California or Maryland. They'd recently eliminated Florida as being too close to Georgia, and Connecticut on general principles. Anna had too much sad history there; she didn't want Theresa to invest her future and Belle's in a place that had brought her so much unhappiness.

And the bad man could still "hunt" there. She'd watched the headlines for years after she'd gotten free, even hired a clipping service, but she hadn't found his trail. The thought of little Belle being snatched by a stranger was too black to contemplate.

"What do you need?" Anna replied as she rounded the corner.

Theresa gave her a sheepish look. "I think I

need more diapers. I'll be glad to go into town if you'll watch Belle,'' she added quickly.

Anna took one look at Belle's little naked butt waiting for the last clean diaper and frowned at Diva, who'd taken up guard duty on the floor under the makeshift crib they'd put together. Then she spoke to Theresa. ''You're supposed to be resting and recovering. I think you'd better watch Belle, and Diva can watch you. I'll go into town for the diapers.''

''Are you sure?'' Theresa asked.

More than you'll ever know, Anna thought. The idea of being solely responsible for Belle's welfare made her heart beat erratically. No one except her dogs had ever depended on her, and her dogs were full grown. ''I have a few other things to pick up anyway,'' she said.

She took Hunter along for the ride. He'd seemed a little flummoxed by the houseful of females, especially one who cried loud enough to be heard in the next county. The first time Belle had exercised her lungs and her God-given right to let everyone know she wasn't happy, the dogs had paced around the house like two parents trying to find the emergency. By now they'd settled into just raising their heads or pointedly coming to Anna to get her to do something about that infernal noise.

Anna patted the big dog sitting next to her in the truck. ''Things have been a lot different lately, haven't they, Hunter?'' Among other things, their regular walks had been curtailed by the arrival of strangers.

Hunter seemed happier than he should be to be away from the house. He didn't respond to her pats; he looked out the window with the concentration of a prisoner on work release.

''It'll get back to normal soon,'' Anna continued. For some reason, that idea didn't appeal to Anna as much as it had a week ago. The trial was coming up. When it concluded, she'd fulfill her promise and make Theresa and Belle disappear, but Anna was beginning to see that she herself would be the loser. She'd changed, more than she'd thought possible.

Everything seemed different since she'd opened her life to Theresa...and to Ben.

Driving along Main Street in Dalton Falls, she passed the Sheriff's Department and felt a hard twist in the vicinity of her heart. Was he still in Atlanta? Or was he busy working on police business? Too busy to worry about her? She'd walked away from him in the moonlight and he'd stayed out of her life. Even knowing she'd done the right thing, Anna wished it had turned out differently.

Better not to wish on the moon. She knew how fickle the moon could be. And how dangerous.

She parked the truck in front of the local grocery store. She'd walk to the drugstore first to get the powder and ointment Juney had recommended to Theresa, not to mention diapers. Then she'd come back for the groceries.

As she and Hunter strode along the sidewalk, she caught herself meeting the gazes of the people she passed. For years she'd looked down, or away. This time, she decided to watch them and wait, to see what they'd do. Some of the men actually nodded a greeting in the traditional mountain way, although most seemed too surprised to do anything but walk by. It could have been the dog. Or, it could have been the Witch of Rain Mountain giving them the evil eye.

Anna almost chuckled as she instructed Hunter to wait at the door of the drugstore. "I'll be right out."

Mission accomplished, Anna thought with satisfaction as she pushed the buggy up the diaper aisle thirty minutes later. If the Dalton Falls drugstore had it in stock, then Anna had loaded it into her basket. She resettled the six packages of newborn diapers after one of them tumbled out and felt an odd sort of contentment.

As she rolled up to the checkout line, however, any good feeling evaporated. The woman behind the counter and the two women lined up in front of her appeared ready to bolt if she so much as spoke. Rather than confronting them as she had the people on the sidewalk, Anna made a great show of perusing the multitude of magazines on the rack near the counter. At no time did she acknowledge anyone's presence and expected them to do the same.

BEN SAW ANNA'S BIG MALE Doberman posted outside the drugstore. He was sitting so still he looked as if he'd been turned into stone. Even so, people on the sidewalk gave the dog a wide berth. He wondered if the dog would remember him, then decided he would walk over and see.

God, he'd missed Anna. And if talking to her dog would give him a glimpse of her, then he'd talk. It had been easy to stay away from her when he'd been out of Dalton Falls, but she'd never left his thoughts. He'd spent most of the night before working out the perfect plan with the perfect reasons to go visit her on Rain Mountain. But he hadn't done it. Seeing her in town was more temptation than he could resist. She was in his territory now.

After jogging across Main Street, he approached from the grocery store since that's where she'd parked her truck. A few folks waved and one car horn honked as he went by, but Ben made a straight line for the drugstore.

He slowed up when he got close. "Hey, buddy, you remember me?" he said to the dog.

The Doberman's head swung toward him but he

didn't move. He didn't look especially friendly, either. Ben's observation that the dog was an assassin in fur came back to nag him. This was one of the few times Ben wished he carried a supply of extralarge dog biscuits. Animals usually understood that feeding meant friend.

Ben walked a few steps closer, within range of those intimidating teeth. "I know Anna. Are you sure you don't remember me?" He squatted down then extended the back of his hand in a slow arc toward the dog's nose. At this point he hoped the dog wasn't particularly hungry.

The big dog remained still, but Ben saw his cropped tail wiggle. Had to be a friendly sign. "You do remember me," he said, and slid his hand over the dog's smooth brow. The dog sniffed his sleeve, and Ben thought they were well on their way to bonding when he heard loud voices coming out of the drugstore. He stood and walked past the dog, putting one hand up to block the sun on the glass. What he saw inside made his temper rise. He pushed through the door.

"I told you, Eldon, I'm not waiting on that woman. What is someone like her doing buying baby things, anyway?"

"You folks have a problem?" Ben asked, keeping his temper under control and keeping his eyes off Anna. He didn't know what he'd do if she looked upset or hurt by the ignorance of these people.

Both the cashier and the owner of the drugstore turned to him.

"No," Eldon said.

"Yes," the cashier disagreed. "Deputy, you tell that...whatever she is, to go somewhere else to shop. She's not welcome here."

"Now wait a minute—" Eldon began.

Unfortunately, Ben met Anna's eyes after the cashier's outburst and saw her cover the hurt with a mocking I-told-you-so look. As if the cashier had proven the point she'd tried to make since he'd known her. Broken. Spoiled. Beyond repair.

Crazy.

To offset the emotion he saw in her gaze, she smiled a cold, calculated-to-creep-someone-out smile. But she didn't move or defend herself.

"Let me tell you how the law works," Ben said, mostly to the cashier but including her boss. "The law says you don't get to decide who's welcome in this store and who's not. The law says if you refuse to serve anyone they can sue the apron off you and shut you down."

"I was trying to tell her that," Eldon cut in.

"Then why don't you give—" he looked at the cashier's name tag "—Irene, her lunch break and ring up the lady's purchases."

"But I don't go to lunch for another hour, and I'm meetin' Dorothy at the diner—"

Both Ben and the store owner stared at her.

"All right, all right," she huffed. "But I'm gonna tell everyone I know about this. Don't you think I won't."

The quiet after she left, except for the beep of the scanner on the register, was a pleasant change. Anna ignored him, and Ben felt little pleasure at forcing the issue with the cashier. Some people would never change. Anna had done her best to show him that. She was strong; she'd probably have gotten what she wanted without him. Problem was, he wanted to help whether she liked it or not.

She paid the druggist with a brand-new one-hundred-dollar bill. He handled it as though it might mutate into a copperhead. Anna's expression remained as chilly as an ax murderer's. Her defense seemed to be scare the hell out of 'em.

Ben picked up two bags of diapers before she could stop him and then, after suffering a cool appraisal, he followed her out the door. When the dog fell into step beside them, Anna asked, "Why didn't you bite him?"

Ben knew she meant him, but he played dumb. "Because he didn't bite me first."

Some of the coldness left her expression when she looked at him. "I'm going to have to train him better."

Several passersby took second looks as the crazy woman, the deputy and the dog made the short trip down the sidewalk to Anna's truck. After the diapers and other supplies had been stowed, Ben used the opportunity to pet the big dog who scared most of the town residents out of their wits. He wasn't above making friends with him to get to his mistress. Anna broke up the reunion, however, by putting the dog in the truck and locking the door behind him.

"I don't think today is the day to leave him on the sidewalk. Someone might do something to him," she said in her distant, businesslike tone.

Ben, startled that she thought so little of the town she'd chosen to live in for five years, had to finally concede her point. They might hurt the dog to teach the owner a lesson.

"Thank you for your help," she said in dismissal, but Ben wasn't ready to be dismissed. He'd been in Connecticut for two days and Atlanta for one and a half—all that time he'd been thinking about Anna. Not this cold stranger the rest of the world saw, but the warm, childlike woman who'd taken up residence somewhere deep inside him. He'd fight anyone who tried to hurt her. Even her.

"I think I'll do a little shopping, too," he informed her before indicating she should go first.

He could have been wrong, but he thought he saw a spark of the real Anna in her eyes before she marched through the door of Anderson's grocery.

ANNA'S INSIDES FELT as if they were caught in a whirlwind. The collision of her two worlds. She'd come to town on an errand for Theresa without giving a second thought to her usual persona, the face she'd hidden behind for the past five years. The Crazy Woman of Rain Mountain.

The women in the drugstore had reacted precisely the way she'd expected the residents of Dalton Falls to. Her cover ruse was in full force. But then Ben had walked in and, so many different emotions had hit her at once, she'd found herself frozen.

It was good to see him, but mortifying as well. Several days had passed since they'd been naked together in the moonlight yet the memory of every taste, every touch, every pleasure came rushing back when she'd looked in his eyes.

And then she'd had to play the witch, to fulfill the part she'd chosen in order to keep everyone at twice a respectable distance. Everyone but Ben.

"How's Theresa?" Ben asked as he pulled a basket free for her to push.

Wanting to get this public display over with as soon as possible since every pair of eyes in the small store seemed to be following her and Ben, she moved into the produce department. "She's fine. She's good with the baby."

After choosing a bag of apples and some lettuce, Anna moved on to the dairy section. She thought she might scream if she didn't get out of there in five minutes or less. Ben followed her with his easy long-legged gait. He obviously wasn't leaving until she did.

"The sheriff said he sent Rudy up to the mountain to check on Theresa." He smiled. "He came back alive, or so I hear."

Anna couldn't meet Ben's eyes. She wondered if the deputy had told him she'd asked about him. The middle of town was the last place she wanted to discuss…them.

"Hunter kept an eye on him, but he stayed in his car," she commented.

"I knew he was a smart man," Ben said with a chuckle.

Feeling overwhelmed by Ben's normalcy in the face of her own turmoil, Anna moved on through the canned foods aisle and the conversation lagged. She was almost halfway finished with her mental list of supplies when they got to the cereal aisle. In the back of the store behind tall shelves, Ben suddenly took her arm and turned her toward him.

If he'd tried to kiss her, she would have pushed him away and run, but he didn't. He looked down at her with a pained and puzzled expression, as if he didn't know what the hell to do either.

"Are you all right, Anna?" he asked.

A bubble of hysterical laughter nearly choked her. She held it in, but barely. To escape his gaze, she lowered her head until her forehead rested against his chest. She could smell the clean, starched smell of his uniform shirt and, underneath, the familiar male smell of his skin. The need to touch him ran through her like a hunger.

"No," she answered into his shirt, "but thanks for asking."

She felt more than heard him laugh. He lowered his mouth until his voice rumbled in her ear. "We need to talk. I'll come up to the cabin later if you promise not to shoot me."

Anna wanted to laugh again. Being close to him was enough to send heat rushing through her from her fingertips to the roots of her hair. She was beginning to comprehend the magnitude of what she'd done. She hadn't simply lost her virginity, she'd made a physical connection with Ben. One that her body would honor even though her mind thought it a bad idea. Not only would she not shoot him, she was liable to make a fool of herself by throwing herself into his arms.

A noise in the next aisle forced Anna to remember where they were. Ben's hand tightened on her arm as if he would keep her close or protect her, but then he eased his grip. With shaking hands, she managed to nod in answer to his question before pushing the buggy farther down the aisle.

THE FIRST THING BEN HEARD when he shut down the engine of his truck in front of Anna's cabin was music. A rich vibration of sound that didn't come from a stereo or radio. He remembered seeing the cello case in Anna's living room. Now he knew without asking that she indeed could play. He got out of the truck, making sure not to slam the door. He didn't want to do anything to interrupt the concert.

The porch step squeaked under his weight and he resisted peeking in the front windows. Surely a knock would set the dogs off. As he paused to decide what to do, the door suddenly opened. Theresa stood on the other side, her baby in her arms, flanked by Anna's dogs. She and the baby had obviously become part of Anna's family.

Anna continued to play.

"Hello, Deputy Ben," Theresa said. "Come in."

As easy as that, Ben, after a polite sniffing from the dogs, entered Anna's cabin and felt as though he'd stepped into a comfortable cave filled with sound.

Anna completed what looked like a particularly

difficult passage of music, then she glanced up at him with a nod.

"Have a seat," Theresa said. "We're trying to get Belle to go to sleep. She loves the cello."

Ben gazed down at the fidgety baby and wondered how Theresa knew what Belle liked or didn't like. The music seemed too loud for a lullaby, but what did he know? The idea of Belle sleeping seemed like a good one though, so he moved to the couch to sit. As he settled on the leather, he noticed the colorful blanket draped across the back and felt a hard tug of recognition. He remembered the same blanket in the moonlight, covering Anna's shoulders before she dropped it and pulled her dress up over her head. The vision of Anna in the moonlight, naked, hit him like a fist. Just then, the cello struck a particularly deep and vibrant note in the music and Ben experienced the vibration from his chest to his groin.

He'd come out here to talk, not to talk her into something. And his immediate reaction had been to picture her naked. He was disgusted, feeling like a thirteen-year-old with his first erection. Ben couldn't look at Anna. She might see how much he remembered, how much he wanted her. He watched her hands instead.

She had beautiful hands.

Within twenty minutes, the dogs were sprawled on the rug at his feet and he felt more relaxed than he had in two weeks. Maybe there was something to this music thing after all.

It seemed the baby thought so. Theresa carefully stood and nodded to Anna. Then, after putting her finger to her lips to shush him, she mouthed goodnight and left the room.

Anna continued to play until she reached the end of the piece. When the music stopped, Ben's whole body tingled with residual vibrations. The sudden silence seemed louder than the cello.

"That was really nice," he said as he watched Anna wipe down the instrument and place it in the case. "You play very well."

Anna snapped the case shut and stretched like a cat, the light from the candles on the mantel haloing her midnight hair. "Thank you." She absently rubbed her hands and fingers. "I used to play with a little more snap, but I don't practice as much as I should."

Ben nodded, having no idea where to go from there. Now that they were done with the obvious topics for conversation, silence settled in once more. Finally Anna plunked her hands down on her knees and faced him.

"Can I get you something to drink? Did you have dinner?"

She was friendlier but still the hostess, not the woman who'd stood up to him, or stretched out over him, naked. Crazy or not, he missed the witch he'd seen in town, the witch he'd made love to in the moonlight.

"No," he said. "I'm fine."

She looked away then, unsure, keeping her gaze anywhere but on him. "I know you said we have to talk, but I don't know how to do this." She stood and paced to the window, turning her back.

Feeling her dismissal like a knife to the chest, Ben stood as well. He could handle her distance in town; he expected it. But not here, in her home where he'd been welcome before. Before he'd touched her, taken her. "Anna?" When she didn't reply, he crossed the room until he was standing behind her. "Anna, please look at me."

When she turned, the witch looked back at him. From the glitter in her eyes to the flare of her nostrils, she was everything he remembered. His heart nearly stopped before charging into double time.

One of her talented hands rose to touch the collar of his shirt. "I know you said we have to talk but—" Her hand shook as she slipped her fingers inside his collar and he covered them with his own.

"We have to—" he began, but he was drawing her closer. Her chin came up as his came down and, without conscious will, he was kissing her.

Her lips were soft and damp and trembling. He determined then and there that the witch was a liar. She wasn't crazy or lost, she was just scared and too alone. And she needed him, for this anyway.

Ben kissed her like she was made of chalk and he was the rain. He formed her mouth under his then reformed it with teeth and tongue. Giving her what she needed and taking what he craved. By the time they came up for air, Anna was molded against him as though they were both fighting the blast of a high wind.

Ben tried to catch his breath, to figure out what he wanted, what they both wanted. Theresa was here, he knew Anna wouldn't leave her to go home with him. Anna's hands were moving over his chest, his neck, his face, making it difficult for him to think. He held her face between his palms to slow her down.

"When we do this again, we're going to do it right."

Anna didn't dispute the "when" in his statement but she looked dazed.

"I want you in a bed—with protection. I want to take my time." He tightened his grip slightly. "And no walking away." He brushed her dark hair back and had the sudden vision of those two barrettes in an evidence bag. Her beautiful hair. His heart sank and he lowered his hands to her shoulders. "Okay?"

She nodded before resting her head on his chest. Ben slipped his arms around her and held her close. He could feel the tension in both their bodies and welcomed it. She wasn't done with him, and he certainly wasn't done with her, not by a long shot.

DEPUTY WALLY DEAN HAD JUST ordered the meat-loaf special from Shirleen at the diner when a stranger sat down next to him. The stranger extended his hand.

"Hi, I'm James Ackerman from the Atlanta News Bureau."

Wally shook the man's hand, assessing his clothes and accent. Not a Georgian, no doubt about that. "I'm Wally Dean, Deputy Dean." Wally was beginning to have a bad feeling that his meal might be interrupted. Since his wife, Jolynne, was out of town, he'd spent all day looking forward to supper at the diner. "What can I do for you?"

Shirleen set down Wally's coffee and offered a cup to the newcomer. He nodded, never taking his gaze from Wally.

"I hear you had a missing girl case up here recently."

Wally thought for a moment, mentally fanning through the cases that were open. No missing girl that he could think of except—

"We had a girl who ran off into the woods after a car wreck, but she turned up. Turns out she was a witness in an unrelated trial. You probably know about that one, being from Atlanta. It's a drug dealer named Jimmy Cintero.'' Wally couldn't help the dig. ''Probably a New Yorker.''

The reporter wrote down the information but he didn't look very happy with it.

''So this case wasn't related to the Annalee Winters case?''

''Annalee Winters?'' Wally said as he watched Shirleen slide his plate of meat loaf and potatoes in front of him. ''I don't guess so. The only Annalee we have around here is Annalee Evans and she's a witch. Isn't that so, Shirleen?'' Wally winked his let's-play-hillbilly wink at the waitress as she topped off his coffee. She took the hint.

''That's right,'' Shirleen said gravely. ''Lives up there on Rain Mountain with man-eating dogs. Shoots anything that moves around her place. We have to clear the sidewalk when she comes down or get the evil eye.''

The reporter didn't look put off by the description. ''How old is this witch, do you figure?''

''Hard to say,'' Shirleen continued. ''We try not to look her full in the face.

''Young or old?'' the reporter persisted. ''Take a guess.''

When Shirleen didn't speak, Wally answered. If they didn't get this conversation over with he'd never get to his meat loaf.

''I'd say somewhere between twenty-five and forty. But if you really want to know about her, you need to ask Deputy Ben Ravenswood. He's been up to her place on the mountain.''

"Ravenswood, you say?" The man looked like he'd hit serious pay dirt. "Thank you, folks," the reporter said, and pulled a twenty-dollar bill from his pocket as he stood. "I'd like to buy your dinner," he said to Wally. "And keep the change," he said to Shirleen.

Finally free to dig into his meat loaf, Wally chewed and watched as the reporter sat outside in his car making calls on his cell phone. He wondered what could be so all-fired interesting about the Witch of Rain Mountain.

LIKE THE ADULTS they were purported to be, Anna and Ben had pulled themselves together—or apart in this case—and settled on the couch to talk.

Anna's nervousness had dissipated and she could only attribute that to Ben. His solid presence seemed to calm her even when his touch excited her beyond common sense. She trusted him, her body trusted him. That's why she'd gone to him in the woods. That's why she would go with him again if he asked. When he asked.

Now, sitting next to him on the couch, thigh to thigh, with his arm behind her shoulders, she felt calm enough to tell him what he wanted to know.

"I told you he didn't rape me," she said, going back to their older conversation.

"I know." Ben rested his big hand on her thigh and she could feel the heat of his skin through her clothes. "Why hasn't there been someone else?"

Anna had no real answer for that except fear… and distrust. "I never let anyone get close enough," she said finally. "I believed that if I let someone into my life, everyone would know my secret and the bad man would find me." She looked up at Ben. "He swore he would find me."

"And you're not afraid anymore? Is that why you came to me?"

She watched him wait for the answer and had to choose her words. She would always be afraid. But not of Ben. She skirted the question with sarcasm. "You trespassed into my life. I couldn't get rid of you." The pained look on his face made her cover his hand with hers. Hurting him unexpectedly hurt her more. "The truth is, there's just something about you. You're as solid as the granite under this cabin. And after what you went through the night of the full moon… I trust you, Ben. I have from the first few times I ran into you in town. You were the one I wanted."

In relief, he turned his hand to grasp hers. "What if we've made a baby?"

"The odds are fairly slim," Anna said to placate him. She had no true idea what the odds were, but after being celibate for so many years surely one sexual encounter wouldn't prove fertile. If she'd

made a mistake, and losing her virginity produced
a child, it would be all the more reason to hide:
from the bad man, from the world, from Ben. The
thought of it sent a tremor of fear down her spine.
She was sending Theresa away to protect Belle,
but the possibility of bringing her own child up in
the world she inhabited scared her beyond reason.

"You'll tell me one way or the other, won't
you?"

Anna gazed into Ben's eyes, the man she trusted
more than any other, and told him a lie.

"I promise."

TRANSCRIPTION of taped session with female minor X, 15 years old. Excerpted from psychiatric
evaluation of Dr. Antony Desillio, Ph.D., State of
New York.

"Why do you say you hate reporters?"

"Because I do."

*"But why? Other than doing their job, what
have they done to you?"*

*"Would you want to be followed everywhere day
and night?"*

*"They don't follow you as much as they used to,
isn't that correct?"*

*"They don't because I stay home. You know
what happened when they couldn't follow me anymore?"*

"No, what happened?"

"One of them poisoned my dog so he could get on the grounds to take pictures of me. He didn't want the dog to bark, you see. So, to do his job, he killed Baker."

"I can see that makes you sad and I understand your feelings. Perhaps your father can buy you another dog to replace Baker."

"No. You don't understand. It doesn't make me sad, it makes me mad. *The next dog I have will have teeth sharp enough to* eat *any reporter who offers him a piece of poisoned meat."*

CHAPTER TWELVE

BY THE DAY BEFORE Jimmy Cintero's drug-trafficking trial, Theresa Smith was well on her way to disappearing. She'd chosen a town in California, Anna's lawyers had put through the reams of legal mumbo jumbo needed to officially start over from zero, and Theresa and Anna had purchased enough furnishings over the Internet to establish a new household with a baby. They'd also bought Theresa several sets of new clothes to be delivered to Dalton Falls, for travel, for court.

Theresa seemed shocked by the money it took to accomplish their plan.

"Can you afford this?" she asked Anna, after twenty thousand dollars had been transferred into Theresa's new bank account.

"I wouldn't have offered if I couldn't."

"But I could get by on a lot less. How can I pay you back?"

Anna turned to face the young girl. "I can afford it. Besides, when you don't have any family in your life to help out, money is the only thing that can keep you safe." She'd been on the run and supporting herself for three years before she could legally claim her inheritance. It had been hard, but she'd done it. In some ways, having so much money had put Anna at risk in the first place. But in other ways, the wealth behind her family name had surrounded her with a buffer of safety. Now she could help Theresa. "You pay me back by going to school and getting a degree. You've got to have a job that pays enough to live in a good neighborhood, to be self-sufficient."

"So I don't get stuck with someone like Jimmy again."

"Exactly."

Theresa hesitated before speaking her mind. "Who made you run away?"

Anna considered refusing to answer, but that had never worked with Theresa in the past. "A man." Her throat felt tight every time she thought of him, because the mental image of his face wouldn't be far behind, followed by the bloody tigers. She fought the debilitating pull of the past. "A bad man."

"Like Jimmy?" Theresa asked.

"No. Much worse than Jimmy," she admitted. "Although if Jimmy is serious about hurting Belle, then I'd put him on the same level."

Memories were closing in, of the other girls the bad man said he had hurt. And, the one fact that

remained constant, he was still out there somewhere. Time to change the subject.

"Now, about tomorrow. Ben said he'll handle
everything. He should be here at seven. We'll take
Belle to Juney's then drive to Atlanta."

"Thank you for coming with me."

It had been a difficult decision. She'd have to
leave her dogs on their own for a night. And after
all the upheaval of the past two weeks, Anna could
have used some time alone, to recharge, regroup.
But Theresa had been especially nervous about
leaving Belle, never mind facing her former boyfriend. Since Anna had stood by her this far, she
wouldn't let her face Jimmy alone in court.

"This will hopefully be the last hard thing you
have to do. After he goes to jail, then you're free."

Theresa didn't look completely convinced. "I'm
glad Deputy Ben is going with us too."

Ben. Anna was glad of that, as well. He'd been
around, calling, stopping by, but he hadn't touched
her, really touched her since the night she'd played
the cello. From the crown of her head to the soles
of her feet, her body didn't care about the reasons
for his absence. Every inch of her wanted Ben. A
shiver of pleasure ran through her at the thought
of being alone with him once this was over.

"Me, too. At least we won't get lost in the Atlanta traffic," Anna said, not the least bit worried.
Traffic was the most minor of their problems. Traf-

fic could only kill you, people could do much worse. "Are you nervous about leaving Belle with Juney?"

Theresa smiled then. "Nah. Not really. I mean I don't like being away from her, but Juney and her daughters know more about babies than I'll ever know. I'm sure she'll be happy there."

"Better them than me," Anna said in heartfelt certainty, expecting Theresa to laugh. But she didn't.

"I would trust you with Belle any day," Theresa said, holding Anna's gaze.

It was Anna who looked away first to hide the rush of emotion Theresa's words caused. If Theresa only knew about her—really knew—she might reconsider. Clearing her throat, she began shutting down the computer. "Well, you shouldn't. I know zip about babies—"

"—and I don't want to learn." Theresa finished for her and she laughed, completely unintimidated by Anna's gruff manner. Then she touched Anna's arm. "Seriously, I hope you have your own someday. You'll be amazed at how it changes the way you look at life, and the future. I know I'll never be the same."

Anna couldn't speak, didn't want to tell Theresa that she never wanted to have someone else to protect from the bad things in the world besides herself and her dogs. She wasn't sure she was up to the job.

Crazy.

She frowned at Theresa. "Thanks to you I'm already a godmother. I think I'll quit while I'm behind."

AT SIX-THIRTY THE NEXT MORNING, Ben stopped at the diner to get some hot coffee for the road. He ran into Wally on his way back to his truck.

"Hey, you taking that girl down to Atlanta today?"

"Yeah, after all the hours we put in looking for her, the sheriff wanted someone to make sure she got there." Ben blew on his coffee before taking a sip.

Wally leaned against the fender of his car and crossed his arms. "Did that news bureau reporter ever talk to you?"

"The what?" Ben asked, a sudden sinking feeling making his coffee taste like acid.

"Some reporter talking about missing girls and an Annalee Winters. Asked what our resident witch looked like. I told him to talk to you." Wally spit on the ground. "He seemed pretty interested, thought for sure he'd call you up. You suppose that woman up on Rain Mountain is a fugitive?"

No. No. No. Ben couldn't have felt worse unless it was picturing himself facing Annalee. The only connection between her real name and Dalton Falls, Georgia, was Ben Ravenswood. How could they have found out about his trip to Connecticut? After fifteen years he'd thought they would have given up. Then he remembered the old news stories he'd read about people being bribed for information, followed, threatened. One of the most famous kidnapping cases since Patty Hearst.

Ben hadn't told a soul, but somehow he'd brought the world to Annalee.

"No, I haven't seen any reporters," Ben finally answered. He threw his full cup of coffee into the trash can sitting at the curb. "If you see the guy, tell him I want to talk to him." He'd talk to him all right. He'd run him out of town before he ever got close to Anna.

Wally seemed puzzled by his change of attitude, but Ben didn't care. He had to warn Annalee and in doing that, he'd have to confess what he'd done.

"What's the matter, coffee not good?" Wally called as Ben got into his truck. Ben dismissed the question with a wave and headed for Rain Mountain.

ANNA WAS AS READY as she'd ever be to go into Atlanta, to walk through the courthouse with its judges and lawyers. The very kind of place and people who had failed her in the past. Today it would be Theresa's turn to have a small measure of justice. She would do her civic duty and testify, then Jimmy would go to jail and Anna would help extricate Theresa from the entire situation. Boom. Gone.

At the expected sound of Ben's truck, Anna opened the front door and stepped out onto the porch. A slight mist still hung in the trees from the cool night. Even though the rising sun turned the mist to gold, summer was nearly at an end. Soon the leaves would begin to turn and she would have to decide to stay one more season or go now.

With her preparations for the trip completed, Anna waited as Ben rolled to a stop, slammed the door to his truck and walked toward her.

"Good morning," she said, trying to put a good face on the beginning of a trip she didn't want to make.

Ben didn't say a word. He walked up the steps and drew her into his arms, then held her, tight. The tenseness in his arms immediately translated trouble.

"What's wrong?" she asked.

"Damn. Damn. Damn," he growled in her ear.

"Ben—" Anna pushed on his chest to look at him. "Tell me."

Ben closed his eyes for a moment then opened them with a sigh. "It's all my fault, I—"

"Is everything okay?" Theresa asked.

Anna turned to find her standing in the doorway

with a full baby bag on one arm and Belle cradled in the other. She looked more frightened than Anna had ever wanted to witness again. And the worst was yet to come.

"Everything is fine," Anna said, stepping out of Ben's reach. "Right, Ben?"

Ben shoved his hands into his pockets. He looked from Anna to Theresa then back to Anna before saying, "Yeah, fine. Let's get going."

As Ben loaded Theresa and the baby into the back seat of his four-by-four, then put the overnight bags in the back, Anna locked the cabin and gave the dogs their orders.

"Now, you have enough food and water here for at least a week if you don't let the possums eat it all. I'll be back tomorrow night. Stay and guard the cabin."

Ben's truck was halfway down the mountain before any of the occupants spoke.

"The dogs didn't look too happy to be left behind," Ben said.

"I just hope no one gets too close to the cabin. If I'm not there to stop them, I don't know what they'll do." Anna had a very good picture of what they'd do since she'd watched them trained. The dog handler had explained that dogs like Diva and Hunter were pretty much the same as having a loaded gun in the house. Care had to be taken so innocent people didn't blunder into something they couldn't handle. Anna considered anyone on her property as, at the least, guilty of trespassing. Their actions would bring the appropriate punishment.

As Ben made the turn onto the main road, a car pulled out behind them. Anna watched Ben study the rearview mirror with more interest than usual. They drove for five miles with headlights behind them until the turn to Juney's left them alone on the road again. Anna tried to relax, but that's when she noticed Ben's grip on the wheel was so tense it made his knuckles white.

THE FEDERAL COURTHOUSE in downtown Atlanta looked like a million other government buildings: cold, from its marble facade, marble floors, to the nearly colorless official government artwork.

Ben, dressed in his uniform, escorted Anna and Theresa up the wide outer steps then through the chrome-framed doors. After a show of ID, he walked around the metal detectors then waited for them on the other side. Together the three of them took the elevator to the third floor, where Theresa had an appointment with the lawyers for the prosecution. Ben and Anna ended up waiting on a bench in a deserted hallway while the lawyers prepared Theresa for her testimony.

Anna didn't waste any more time wondering about Ben's earlier behavior.

"Why have you been so jumpy today?" she

asked as soon as Theresa was out of sight. "Usually I'm the one watching every shadow."

Ben had to admire Anna's courage to be out in the world again after what he'd learned about her past. She was right: for once she almost seemed calm and he hated like hell to spoil her newfound serenity. But he had to tell her, at least part of it. He didn't want the surprise coming from someone else. Knowing there was no time like the present, Ben searched inside for the right words.

"I saw Wally Dean this morning at the diner. He said there was a reporter in town asking about you."

At the word *reporter,* Anna's face changed. All color drained away as she glanced around then past him, as if the man might spring from the carpet. Ben covered her hand with his, feeling even worse about his own stupidity.

"It's okay, Anna. He can't get to you—"

"It's not okay."

He could see her mind working on escape. He squeezed her hand to keep her focused on him. "He was in Dalton Falls. He can't know you're here. When we get back I'll take care of him." He had to make it right, since he was the cause.

It was on the tip of his tongue to tell her it was his fault, to explain that he'd gone to Connecticut to help, except she looked ready to bolt. If she ran from him, there would be no one else to protect her.

"What about Diva and Hunter? If someone goes to my cabin—"

Ben had no doubt that the dogs could take care of any reporter who might be stupid enough to face them, but he knew Anna worried about her guardians. "I'll call and tell Rudy to drive up there and check on the place. He knows to stay in the car. Would that make you feel better?"

Anna nodded then said, "Tell him not to try to feed them."

He didn't question the oddness of the request. He watched as her mind shifted to other matters. For the fortieth time since he'd met Annalee, he would have paid good money to know what she was thinking.

ANNA WAS STRUGGLING NOT TO CRY. *They've found me.* She'd been considering the necessity of moving on but had put off the decision because of Theresa…because of Ben. Now the decision had been taken out of her hands.

A reporter.

Where there was one, several more usually followed, and then, there'd be a relentless free-for-all. She'd had a good run in Dalton Falls. Five years since the last move. If Ben was right, the word wouldn't get out about her whereabouts for a few days yet. Reporters usually wanted to keep a hot story to themselves until they had what they wanted to run—descriptions, exclusive pictures.

There was still time to send Theresa and Belle on their way, but she needed to set her own move in progress. She already knew the next destination. Anna gazed up into the serious face of the man who'd come to mean more to her than any other and wondered how she could say goodbye.

There wouldn't be time now, though. Ben glanced over her shoulder and said, "Here comes Theresa."

The next few minutes were spent with one of the lawyers, who explained to Anna and Ben that Theresa would testify the next day and that she had to be in the courtroom by nine in the morning. Anna made a valiant attempt to keep her expression neutral, but as soon as the lawyer left them, Theresa looked at her and asked, "What's wrong?" A sad testament on the girl's life, expecting disaster at every turn. Not unlike Anna herself.

Anna stood to avoid Theresa's assessing eyes. How had this teenager gotten past all her barriers in such a short time? She must be losing her touch. "I don't know what you mean," she answered.

Theresa backed up and stared at the two of them. "You guys are scaring me." She faced Ben. "Tell me why she's upset. It's your fault, isn't it?"

Ben looked so stricken that Anna stepped in to fend off Theresa's assumptions. She took the girl's arm and walked her a short way down the hall. Anna faced her, then pushed back several strands of Theresa's blond hair before speaking. "Remember I told you that when there's a tear in your safety net you have to move on?" Theresa nodded. "Well, I just found a tear in mine."

Fear tainted Theresa's features but she remained resolute. "Will you be able to stay with me until tomorrow?"

Anna nodded. "We should have a few days before things get out of hand. Time enough to get you and Belle on your way."

"It isn't fair," Theresa said, eyes filling with tears.

"No, it isn't. But it's the best you and I can do. Okay?"

The girl sniffed then visibly pulled herself together. "Okay."

Anna waved Ben forward and included him in the conversation. She'd put the fear aside. She could deal with this as she had so many times in the past. Disappearing. There were logical steps to take, ways to get lost and stay lost in a crowd. She needed a telephone and a little time.

"Ben, you need to make your phone calls to Dalton Falls from the pay phones here at the courthouse. What hotel are we booked into?"

"The Radisson. It's close."

"I'll make some new reservations under a different name."

Ben seemed reluctant. "I have a lot of friends on the force here, I'm sure I could get some of them to help out."

"No." Anna said. "You can't contact any of them. We have to do this alone."

"But I know these men, they're professionals."

"Ben—" she touched his arm "—I knew every one of the people who betrayed me in the past— lawyers, police, friends…family. It's the three of us, or nothing."

That seemed to end the argument and Anna was supremely grateful, because the next course of action would have been that she and Theresa get lost on their own. Anna wasn't ready to give up Ben yet, even though she knew now, without a doubt, that she had to disappear, and disappear quick.

THEY'D ORDERED DINNER in their rooms at the Ritz Carlton. After eating but barely tasting the food, Ben, dressed in an old pair of sweats and a T-shirt, paced across the luxurious carpet of his room without enjoying it. When he'd asked Anna why she'd chosen the Ritz, she'd said because most reporters couldn't afford the room rates, so the chances of them bumping into anyone who might recognize Anna were slimmer. The depth of her experience with being on the run made him want to punch something.

And now she'd gone into hiding because of his stupidity.

He wished he could go and talk to her, confess everything and convince her he could help. Somehow he could make things right. But she and Theresa had taken to their room like two criminals being chased by bloodhounds and he had no way to ease their worries. And no real way to help. Anna seemed to know more about this than he did.

He rested a forearm against the window looking out over the sparkling lights of Buckhead. He knew Anna had erased her past at least once before. Her official records began five years ago. Before that, Annalee Evans had not existed. He had no doubt she could do it again. What was she doing—planning? Would she even tell him when the time came?

Unable to stand the silence any longer, he shoved away from the window and headed for the door. He'd go to her and Theresa's room and make them tell him their plans. The thought of Anna out in the world with no way to find her was... unacceptable.

As his hand covered the doorknob, a knock made the door vibrate. When he opened it, he found Anna standing on the other side as though she'd heard his frustration. Without greeting, he pulled her through the door, closed it, and held her as if she might take off any second. Neither of them spoke.

Anna rested calmly in his embrace, but her posture was a little stiff. Ben's guilt clogged his throat and he could barely swallow, let alone confess or apologize.

"It's gonna be okay," he finally managed to say.

"I know," Anna replied. She leaned back and looked up at him. Her amber-colored eyes were clear, as though she'd shaken off any indecision, and she mapped his face like a woman who wanted to remember.

"As soon as we get back to Dalton Falls, I'll take care of that reporter," he vowed. And he would. He could get away with a little police harassment in Wayne County, he was a native son.

She smiled slightly. "I don't want to talk about it anymore tonight," she said. She touched his cheek with her hand. "Remember saying 'when we do this the next time'?"

He nodded.

"How about now?"

Frustration and lust warred inside Ben. He needed to know what she was thinking, but as his fingers moved along her arms, he got caught up in the feeling, the touching. His logical mind beginning to scramble, he fought the distraction of having her in his arms.

"Ben?" She gazed at him expectantly.

He couldn't hold in the question. "Are you planning to leave with Theresa when she goes?"

She didn't hesitate. "No."

"Will you tell me what you are planning?"

"No."

So, this is it, Ben thought. One last goodbye— just the two of them, alone. A man with more pride might have refused. A policeman with more leads on her kidnapper might have promised he'd solve the case and save her from her nightmares. But Ben had lost what was left of his ragged heart to Annalee and he would never tell her no or make promises neither of them could keep.

He pulled her close again to escape those rational eyes and sighed into her hair. "Do you know I'd do just about anything for you?" he asked.

She nodded but remained silent.

"Do you know I would kill anyone who tried to hurt you?"

Again she nodded.

"Do you know how much it's going to hurt to let you go?"

She pushed back then and gazed into his eyes once more, but he could see there would be no last-minute reprieve, no hopeful lies. "We have some time yet. Let's spend it together."

ANNA WATCHED THE STRUGGLE on Ben's face and felt her rock-solid resolve waver. She could tell Ben her plans; he wouldn't hurt her, not on purpose. She trusted him. But the shock of the past catching up with her had shoved aside any of the relaxed feelings she'd experienced in the past week. She didn't know how they'd found her, but they had. Because of that, she had to force herself back into the focused mind-set of the hunted in order to do what had to be done. In order to leave Dalton Falls, her cabin, her name, her life.

Ben.

Otherwise, sooner or later, the bad man would find her. She wasn't a child anymore. She wouldn't obey, hoping to change his mind. A confrontation at this point in her life would leave one of them dead. She'd been trained to defend herself, learned how to shut down her emotions and do what had to be done. She'd never be taken again.

Anna closed her eyes and slipped her arms around the warm solidness of Ben. Above all else, she didn't want her fear of the past to interfere with this night. Ben was the one happy surprise in her life. She wouldn't give him up until she had to.

"Kiss me, Ben. Please."

Ben's mouth was warm and surprisingly gentle since the tremor in his arms betrayed his impatience. It was so like him to be gallant, to be careful. Before allowing herself to follow those thoughts to softer feelings, Anna caught his bottom lip with her teeth and tugged. She wasn't a child or a virgin anymore; she wanted him to know he didn't have to be careful. Not this time.

After hearing one surprised intake of breath, she let go. He licked his lip, then hers before nipping her back. Then heat took over. As Anna relinquished her fears and her plans to the pleasure of a hot, openmouthed kiss, she fought to forget about anything other than the magic they'd found between them.

Her clothes drifted to the bed and the floor without her help, and soon she and Ben were stretched out on the pristine white sheets of the king-size bed, naked.

"This is a big step up from a sleeping bag," Ben teased, as his mouth caught hers again. A long, wet kiss sent Anna's body into an overload of need. She couldn't imagine anything feeling as wonderful as Ben, whether on satin sheets or rough ground.

"This is much better than most everything," she concluded.

His mouth settled over then sucked one of her nipples, causing her to arch upward. She was beyond speaking now, didn't want to explain or direct. She wanted to live in his touch, in this moment. And she wanted to remember.

Ben seemed determined to fulfill his promise to take his time, do this right. The only part of Ben's declaration she couldn't agree to was the "no walking away." Maybe she *could* agree. She wasn't going to walk, she was going to run.

One of Ben's legs slid over hers and nudged her thighs apart. Running went totally out of her brain as his hand slid over the most private part of her. For a second the image of the bad man touching her intruded on her excitement and a tiny thread of panic caused her to jump.

Ben's hand froze. "Are you okay?" he asked, sounding out of breath and too far gone to stop.

Anna made a quick survey of exactly how she felt, having Ben looming over her, touching her, holding her down with his leg.

She felt fine. Better than fine, she wanted this. Nothing about Ben's touch reminded her of the past—nothing. It was simply her mind playing tricks.

She covered Ben's warm, gentle hand with her own and pressed him to her. "I'm excellent. I want you to touch me."

"Do you want to be on top?"

Anna gazed up at his earnest face, into his hazel eyes and told the truth. "No, there's no moon. It's just you and me."

FAIRFIELD, CONNECTICUT, police announcement to the press on the second anniversary of Annalee Winters's abduction.

Due to a lack of evidence and/or witnesses, there have been no arrests or viable leads in the kidnapping case involving Annalee Winters. After two years of diligent and top-priority status, the case has been declared inactive awaiting further information. Every effort has been made and will continue to be made to close this case.

CHAPTER THIRTEEN

As Ben let the warm shower pummel his face and head the next morning, he fought the feeling of impending doom that had settled over him.

Anna.

She'd stayed with him most of the night before insisting she had to return to her room to dress for court. Ben was convinced he'd just spent the most incredible night of his life with the woman who'd captured his heart.

And now that night was over.

She'd touched him and kissed him and held him as though they'd never be apart, or never be together again. Her eyes couldn't lie. She would leave and he wouldn't know where or how she was. It was enough to make a saint into a sinner, or a man into a raving lunatic.

Lunatic. This was all the kidnapper's fault. Working as a police officer, Ben was used to the immediacy of solving a crime, of dealing with criminals. But afterward, harried by new crimes and new cases, no one gave much thought to the victims. They were supposed to be satisfied by the justice the courts handed out. Knowing Anna had taught him about lives broken, by the whim of a sick mind. No justice could mend that.

Ben hoped the man would have his own private corner in prison or in hell when his time came. A corner where the hunters of the world could catch him, where he would have no place to run or hide.

Run and hide.

Ben abruptly shut the shower off and rubbed the water out of his eyes. *You big dope! She isn't running from the reporters, or strangers. She's running from* him. *She thinks he's still out there looking for her. Think. Think.* What had the police overlooked? There had been one other abduction somewhat like Anna's two years after she'd escaped. Then, nothing. He grabbed a towel and headed for the phone. It was a slim chance, but he had to try it. He dialed directory assistance and asked for the Fairfield, Connecticut, police department.

As Theresa French-braided Anna's hair, Anna filled her in on what might happen in court.

"When we go in, there will probably be a few reporters outside. You'll walk with the lawyer, let him do the talking. If there are any photographers, try to keep your head down or turned. The fewer people who see what you look like, the better. Pictures can come back to haunt you years later."

"Where will you be?" Theresa's voice sounded small, subdued.

Anna raised a hand and touched her arm. "I'll be right behind you. But there are already too many people who know we're connected. No use making the connection public."

"Are we connected?" Theresa asked as she finished the braid and tied it off.

Anna scooted over on the bed and pulled Theresa down next to her. She put an arm around the girl's thin shoulders and sighed dramatically. "Yes, I'm afraid we are. As much as I tried to scare you off. You just stuck like a tick and now look at us."

Theresa didn't react to the humor. Anna decided on the truth. "I consider you my friend. The first real friend I've ever had." The statement surprised even Anna. Theresa had come to her for help yet asked for very little. She wasn't after Anna's money, or a way to cash in on her past. She didn't want to hear the lurid details of dark nights under the full moon. She wanted and needed a friend to stand by her and she'd been willing to do the same for Anna.

Anna was shocked when she blinked and tears spilled down her own cheeks. "I'm gonna miss you," she confessed before rubbing the tears away. "And before you ask why, the answer is because."

Theresa gave one sob of laughter then threw her

arms around Anna's neck. They hugged each other hard for a moment, then they were interrupted by a knock at the door.

"Come on, now," Anna said, making an attempt at lightness and encouragement. "That'll be Ben. Let's go put the bad guy in jail so you can get back to Belle."

THE COURTHOUSE HALLS WERE moderately crowded as they made their way to Courtroom four. As she'd planned, Anna hung back allowing first Ben, then one of the lawyers to escort Theresa to her appointed place.

Anna had dressed in a tailored suit and had Theresa braid her hair into a subdued style hoping to blend in with the lawyers and legal aides. Determined to keep her promise, however, she never strayed far from Theresa, though her edginess had returned full force. Except for the few glorious hours she'd spent in Ben's arms the night before, she'd been on guard. She wasn't sure what was coming...she just knew it would.

Two people standing in the open doorway had halted the progress of the people entering the courtroom. Theresa's lawyer stepped ahead to clear the path. That's when a tall, rawboned woman with blondish-gray hair moved out of the crowd and grabbed Theresa's arm.

"There you are, you ungrateful slut!"

Stunned for a moment, Theresa didn't react. Then, looking terrified, she used both hands to try pushing the woman away. Anna charged forward in time to hear the woman screech.

"What did you do with that baby? Kill it?"

The woman's grip was ironlike, but Anna's anger gave her the strength to peel her fingers away. "Leave her alone!" Just as she dislodged the woman's hand, a camera flashed, once, then again. Everyone seemed to be talking at the same time.

"Clear this doorway!" Ben's voice boomed over the others. "Right now."

People started moving, but the woman stood her ground. Theresa seemed morbidly caught in her spell—as if she was staring down a rattlesnake, too terrified to run.

"Ma'am, if you have no business in this courtroom, I'll have to ask you to leave. If you refuse, I'll have to arrest you." Ben's voice sounded official.

The woman never took her beady eyes off Theresa, and Anna suddenly had a terrible, sinking feeling.

"Of course I have business here. This is my girl. I came to watch her make liars and fools out of all of us."

Anna lost her cool then. "You don't know what you're talking about!"

The woman smiled, an eerie, malicious smile.

She glanced around to make sure everybody had their eyes on her. "It's you who don't know. I'm her mama. She said she's mad at her boyfriend for puttin' that baby in her belly then not marrying her. That's why she's here in court like a tattletale. Well, I'm here to tell you she don't know who put that baby in her. Could have been her own daddy if you ask me!"

Theresa had gone completely white and, as she shook her head, she swayed on her feet.

Anna felt Ben's hand on her arm. He put his free arm around Theresa and ushered them both into the courtroom, away from that horrible woman. He found them a seat as close to the prosecution as possible, Theresa in the corner, then Anna next to her, then he took a seat next to Anna. Anyone who wanted to harass the witness would have to get past an officer of the law and the Witch of Rain Mountain.

Anna could feel Theresa trembling from head to toe. She took the girl's right hand in both of hers and squeezed.

"It isn't true," Theresa whispered, looking down as though every once of strength had been drained out of her.

"I know it isn't," Anna said automatically, not even knowing which of the accusations they were discussing. Anna figured a woman like that, who enjoyed tormenting her own flesh and blood in front of an audience, had to be lying.

"I expected I'd have to face Jimmy—" she swallowed to steady her voice "—but I didn't expect her to be here."

"Are you sure she's your mother?"

Theresa's mouth trembled and she almost smiled. "That part is true."

"Damn."

When the bailiff came to escort Theresa to the judge's office to wait, she stood with her head held high and followed him from the room. The trial itself was almost anticlimactic compared to the excitement in the hallway. In some ways, Theresa's mother had done her a favor. By the time the girl was called to testify, she'd regained her composure and had even worked up a little righteous anger. Anna watched as Theresa gave the testimony the D.A. wanted concerning Jimmy Cintero's drug-trafficking activities with special attention to the aggravated assault with a deadly weapon charge.

Theresa only looked once at Jimmy, sitting stoically at the defense table dressed in a brand-new suit and tie, and a shiver seemed to go through her. Immediately she shifted her gaze to Anna. Then she sat up a little straighter and continued answering questions.

Cross-examination was difficult but, again, Theresa's mother had prepared them for anything. So, when the accusations came from the lawyer's mouth, the venom was too weak to cause pain.

Eventually Theresa had her vindication. Dismissed after her testimony, she was allowed to sit in the courtroom to hear the remaining witnesses. When her mother was called to testify—on Jimmy's behalf—the woman also had to be cross-examined. And the lawyers for the prosecution, one of whom had witnessed the hallway incident, goaded her until she became openly abusive and had to be dismissed. But not before the prosecution established the fact Jimmy Cintero had paid Theresa's mother to keep the girl quiet or to make her look like a liar.

BY LUNCH, which came before closing arguments, Anna and Theresa had done everything they could to make the trial a success and obviously wanted to get back to Dalton Falls. Ben had to admire the surprising toughness of these two fragile-looking women. They'd just been through hell. As he'd been led from the courtroom, the defendant Jimmy Cintero had looked both of them over with a chilling half smile. Ben shook his head at the memory. Clutching Anna's hand, Theresa had held her boyfriend's gaze without faltering. Anna herself had actually smiled back at him defiantly. Whoever had claimed women were the weaker sex had no idea what he was talking about.

The lawyers for the prosecution felt confident they would get a conviction and, with Jimmy Cintero's lengthy rap sheet, some serious time seemed inevitable. They congratulated Theresa on her coherent testimony and promised to relay the verdict and any other pertinent information about sentencing.

Fighting the urge to put his arm around Anna and Theresa, Ben followed them to the double doors at the back of the courtroom. He'd be glad to have this business behind him. He had other things to worry about, like Anna. Most of the spectators had already left, for lunch or other business. Theresa was just remarking that she'd been dreaming about Burger King Whoppers for a week when they pushed through the doors.

The sight that met them had Ben blinking to make sure he wasn't dreaming himself. At least fifty people were gathered in the hallway, some with cameras, others with microphones—all apparently waiting for them.

Anna froze for a few seconds, then, as if it was second nature she reached into her bag, brought out a pair of very dark glasses and slipped them on. Flashes were going off like fireworks. She nudged Theresa to the right, toward the elevators, and the crowd descended like a wave.

"Miss Winters? Aren't you Annalee Winters?"

"Where have you been all these years, Miss Winters? Is it true you were institutionalized?"

"Have they found the man who kidnapped you, Miss Winters?"

Theresa seemed mesmerized by them. Anna kept her moving. "Don't look at them," was all she said.

Theresa immediately shielded her face with her hand. Ben felt helpless. He did his best to warn reporters away, but when a few stopped, the others surged around them.

When it became obvious waiting for an elevator would be impossible, Anna gestured for Theresa to follow. The two of them disappeared behind the first door past the elevators and Ben placed himself in front of it.

"I don't know what you're looking for, but you aren't going to find it here," he said, wondering how in Hades he would be able to get Anna and Theresa out of the building without reinforcements.

"Isn't that Annalee Winters, the heir to the Winters fortune?"

"Is she involved in the Jimmy Cintero trial?"

Ben did his best to imitate the sphinx, but he was getting too angry to remain inscrutable.

"Back off," he warned.

He stood like Anna's big dog, guarding her and the door for another fifteen minutes. The questions coming from the reporters slowed and a few members of the group left to file stories or deliver the film they'd shot. Ben waited a few moments longer then slipped through the door.

It turned out to be an empty office. He found Annalee talking on the telephone while Theresa paced near the desk. As soon as the door closed behind him, someone tried to push it open. Ben flattened his hand against the wood and shoved, hard, feeling a small amount of pleasure from the bang and the curse he heard echo in the crowded hallway. He hoped he'd given someone a bloody nose. It was the least he could do for Anna. He locked the door, feeling better already.

"I'll have to call downstairs for some help," Ben began.

Anna held up a hand to interrupt. "That'll be fine," she said into the phone. "We'll be there in forty minutes." She hung up without saying goodbye.

Ben didn't like the distant, businesslike expression on her face.

"We have to go," she said without preamble. She picked up her bag and moved around the desk. The only sign of emotion came as she put a hand on his arm. "This door—" her voice wobbled as she tilted her head "—leads into an empty courtroom. Theresa and I will go out that way, down the stairs."

Ben realized they'd stumbled into one of the

judges' offices. Surely the press wouldn't dare enter without permission. "But—"

"I've already called a cab to meet us downstairs. We'll take it to the airport and rent a car to drive back to Dalton Falls."

The airport. It was damned hard to take care of Anna when she was so efficient at taking care of herself. He knew without asking that he wasn't going with them. He had to be the decoy and drive his truck back later. Without pausing to think or worry, Ben squeezed Anna's hand, gave her a quick kiss then looked her in the eye. "Let them see you in here when I open the door, then take off." She nodded.

Ben waited until Theresa and Anna were standing behind him before opening the door and stepping out. The remaining reporters immediately perked up and lights came on. "Miss Winters? Could we speak to you a moment about—" Ben shut the door hard, crossed his arms like a bodyguard with an attitude and blocked the entrance.

AFTER WATCHING CLOUDS OVERTAKE the sunset, Anna and Theresa made it home to Dalton Falls. They had to contend with detours and traffic, and Anna had insisted on stopping for lunch. She reminded Theresa of the lesson the girl had learned running through the woods, pregnant, without food or the proper clothing: It was difficult to escape or outsmart anyone if you didn't take care of yourself. Eat lunch, eat dinner, sleep.

Run away, run away, hide.

Anna was a little surprised at how easily she'd slipped back into flight mode. She took in the passing scenery like a stranger already viewing the past. No more walking the fence line in the woods, no more feeling at "home." No more wondering what it would be like to fit into this town, or any town for that matter. No more listening for the sound of Ben's truck coming down the driveway. Dalton Falls would become history for her and the dogs as soon as Theresa was on her way.

Theresa had breathed a sigh of relief when they'd picked up Belle. Considering the threats and stress of the past few days, Anna imagined the girl had to see for herself that her daughter was fine. For once, Juney had little to say. She'd hugged Theresa, kissed Belle on the head, then she'd gazed into Anna's eyes for several uncomfortable seconds. With a nod of inevitability, she walked them to the door.

When they reached the other side of Rain Mountain, the dogs were suspicious of the rental car until Anna rolled down the window and called to them. Then they practically leaped for joy, circling the car before shamelessly begging for attention. Smiling, Anna greeted her two unwavering friends with hugs and pats. No matter what occurred, it was nice to have someone in her life who was always glad to see her.

Fat raindrops were falling by the time Anna and Theresa, with armloads of baby paraphernalia, made it under the cover of the porch. Dog food crunched under their feet as Anna unlocked the front door.

"I can see you guys had a party while I was away," Anna said as she switched on the porch light.

"More like a food fight," Theresa commented as she took Belle inside.

Within an hour order had been restored, dinner begun and Theresa settled in Juney's rocking chair to nurse Belle. She looked up as Anna entered the living room.

"I'm gonna miss this place," she said.

Anna glanced around at her home, the one she had designed and built into a perfect sanctuary. "Me, too," she said, then shrugged, knowing she could build another. All the important things, her books, her dogs, her cello would go with her. Everything but her first friend, her first goddaughter and Ben, her first lover.

"When should I leave?" Theresa asked.

Since she didn't detect any hesitation, Anna answered matter-of-factly, "I thought you could take the rental back to the airport day after tomorrow. You have the tickets, the key to the deposit box, and by then we should know the outcome of the trial and sentencing.''

Theresa nodded. They'd gone over the details several times. Anna had watched Theresa practice signing her new name for bank cards and credit cards, until they both knew it by heart.

Anna went to her desk and removed a manila folder. ''Everything is in here—Belle's birth certificate, a new one for you, instructions for when you arrive and several names—a doctor and people who will help you get settled.

''If you need me, need anything, you know who to contact. Remember what I told you to say?'' Anna asked.

A crack of thunder rumbled around the mountaintop and Belle shifted in her mother's arms.

Theresa nodded again. ''Jimmy's back in town.''

BEN DROVE HOME through the rainstorm, cursed with low visibility and way too much time to think. He'd spent the afternoon decoying reporters. They seemed to think that he would sooner or later lead them to Annalee. He'd had a graphic example of what she'd had to live with for so long. Being shadowed and watched. He remembered Annalee slipping on a pair of dark glasses as if she'd been pursued hundreds of times. Hell, he'd have gone postal years before if he'd had to survive as a celebrity.

But Annalee had nerves of steel…and a shotgun.

His first impulse was to drive straight up Rain Mountain to make sure Anna and Theresa had really come back to Dalton Falls. It crossed his mind that they could have gotten on a plane at the airport and already been halfway to anywhere. He had the perfect excuse to go to Annalee's; he still had their overnight bags in his truck. He had business first, though. He'd made some calls earlier and he hoped he'd have some answers soon.

As he made the turn onto the square, headed toward the Sheriff's Department, he noticed there were more than the usual number of cars parked along Main Street. When he got to the Department Only parking lot, that "too little, too late" thing bit him, hard. He parked his truck and hurried through the rain toward the back entrance reserved for officers, dreading what he might find inside.

It was worse than he'd imagined. The sheriff and Wally Dean were holding a mini press conference for about twenty or so newspeople.

"As I was saying," the sheriff repeated, "Miss Evans or Winters is a private citizen with rights like any of the rest of you. I can't give you any information that isn't public record." He turned and pinned Deputy Dean with a stern look. "Any other information is unsubstantiated gossip no matter what the source.'' Then the sheriff noticed Ben standing in the hallway.

"Some of you requested to speak to Deputy Ravenswood, and he's here.''

There was a general shuffling among the reporters, and again Ben had the feeling of being pursued. How had she stood it?

"Deputy? Do you have anything to say to these people?''

He almost refused. He wanted to shout, "Why don't you leave her alone? She's the victim here, not the criminal!'' But none of that would help Annalee. In fact, it might make things worse. He nodded to the sheriff and made his way across the room.

"Deputy, what is your relationship with Annalee Winters?''

"What exactly do you mean?'' He put on his best cop-dealing-with-a-mob face.

"Your relationship...you know...are you close?''

"I know a woman named Annalee Evans, just like I know most of the other citizens of Dalton Falls.''

"What about all these stories of her being a witch? Are any of those true?''

Now Ben knew why the sheriff had shot Wally the angry look. "I think some folks around here have a little too much imagination. I've been up to her property and haven't seen any evidence of witchcraft or any other cult.''

For a split second the vision of Anna under the moon, naked and holding a knife seared his brain. He almost lost it. He coughed to cover the crumbling wall of his defense. He'd never been very good at lying, because he didn't believe in it— even though sometimes, like the present, it was the best policy.

''Where exactly is her place?'' One of the reporters asked and the rest seemed to hold their collective breath.

Ben dug up a cynical smile. ''Now do you boys think because we live up here in the mountains that we don't have the brainpower God gave a jackass?'' His Southern accent practically dripped down the walls.

The reporter grinned. ''Can't blame me for trying.''

''I want to ask all of you a question now.'' Ben crossed his arms and went on. ''I want to know why you're chasing someone you think *might* be someone else. Someone who was the victim of a crime over a decade old?''

He was met with silence.

''Well?''

''The public loves this kind of stuff. They want to know what happened to the poor little rich girl who was kidnapped,'' one of them answered. Several others nodded. "The story is even better if she's joined a cult or become mentally unstable. There were rumors at the time that she'd been committed."

Ben would never understand the value of dragging such sad events up again after fifteen years—true or not. Making a living off someone else's misery and misfortune seemed almost as heinous as kidnapping. "What happens if you've caught up with the wrong woman and you trample over her rights to get a story that isn't true?"

"Then we go home," one of them said.

"Well then, go home," Ben instructed. "You've got the wrong woman."

"Deputy, are you saying that you know for a fact that this woman isn't Annalee Winters? That you have evidence?"

Working not to lose his official calm, Ben spoke slowly and succinctly. "There's no such thing as evidence that someone *isn't* who you think they are. Only the other way around. But yes, I know for a fact this woman isn't the woman you're looking for."

"How do you know?"

"I saw her fifteen minutes ago and she told me so."

"Could you give us a better description of her?"

"No. And that's all I have to say." He walked away, hearing his name called along with a few other questions. He had to leave or lose it. Behind him, the sheriff and Wally were telling them the question-and-answer time was over. He made it down the hall to his desk without being stopped. There were at least forty phone messages stacked near the phone. Had to be reporters. But one could be what he was waiting for. As he started to go through them, there was a knock on the door. The sheriff opened it and stuck his head in.

"Don't shoot. I'm one of the good guys." He moved into the room and shut the door behind him before settling in a chair.

"That was something out there. Looks like we've got ourselves a bona fide celebrity." He rubbed his chin and grinned. "I hate it when that happens. What are we gonna do about it?"

Ben sighed. "I don't know. It's my fault, you know. They tracked her through me. Somebody up in Connecticut talked to the press about my 'unofficial' visit."

"Speaking of that. You got a call today and I took it. Didn't want to write anything down since it was the FBI and the reporters were already all over us. It was the profiling unit. They said they're working on the information and would get back to you as soon as they knew something."

"It's a shot in the dark, but it's all I've got," Ben admitted.

The sheriff stood and slapped him on the shoulder. "You'd be amazed how many targets have been hit by a shot in the dark. Men, too." He turned to leave then stopped. "Oh, and what do you think we ought to do about Wally and his flappin' jaw? You think it would teach him a lesson if I put him on midnight shift where there's precious few to talk to?" The sheriff chuckled. "It would serve him right. JoLynne would be mad for a year."

After the sheriff left, Ben read through the rest of the messages then tossed them all into the trash. He'd waited long enough. He picked up the phone and called Annalee.

"Hello?"

His heart did a slow flip-flop at the sound of her voice. She was still on Rain Mountain.

"It's Ben."

She breathed a sigh into the phone and Ben could almost hear her relax.

"Hey, Ben, are you okay?"

"That's supposed to be my question. You made it back without problems?"

"Yeah, we even missed the rain. Are you coming out?"

Ben closed his eyes and rubbed the ache on one side of his head. "No. I—" He couldn't lie to her. "I know I have your luggage in my truck, but this place is crawling with reporters. If I even look in that direction, they'll be up there on my heels."

There was a longer silence than Ben could stand. "I'm sorry, Annalee. I'm the one who led them here—"

"It's not your fault," Anna said, but the friendliness had vanished. He knew without seeing her face that she'd shifted back into the stranger who kept her distance. She'd said that everyone had failed her, now he had been added to the list. "Don't worry about the bags, we don't need them."

Ben squeezed his eyes shut then rubbed the itchiness of emotion away. He'd thought he could save Annalee, but all he'd done was make things much worse. Feeling more helpless than he had the night Sharon had died, Ben only had one more card to play.

"Please promise you won't leave until you talk to me. I have something I'm working on that might help."

"I don't need help, Ben. It only brings me trouble. But I thank you for wanting to try. I'll be here until Friday evening—after I get Theresa on her way."

"Promise you won't leave without saying goodbye," Ben said again.

"I promise."

IT WAS THE SECOND TIME she'd lied to Ben. Anna hung up the phone feeling at least a hundred years old. How in the world would she survive being pursued for the remainder of her life? It hadn't occurred to her until this moment that someday she'd be too old or too tired to run anymore. What would happen then?

After keeping every other human being at arm's length, there wouldn't even be anyone to offer help. She'd be what she'd always wanted to be—since the kidnapping anyway—alone. No Ben, no-body.

Belle started to cry, which brought her back to the present. Anna felt like crying along with her. As Theresa rocked the baby, Anna went over to the cello case and took out the instrument. Perhaps she could play and make the three of them feel a little better.

TRANSCRIPTION of taped session with female minor X, 16 years old. Excerpted from psychiatric evaluation of Dr. Antony Desillio, Ph.D., State of New York.

"What do you want to be when you grow up?"

"I am grown-up."

"I'm sorry, you're right. I meant when you finish school, go out on your own. What do you want to do with your life?"

"I want to live by myself in a place where nobody knows me."

"Why?"

"So that no one can tell him where I am."

"It's been two years now, do you really think he's still out there looking for you?"

(Sigh)

"I've told you over and over again that he swore he would find me."

"Why do you still believe him?"

"Because he's the only one out of all of you—the police, the doctors, my friends…my father—who told me the truth."

CHAPTER FOURTEEN

THE ATLANTA NEWSPAPER HAD PUT Anna's picture on the front page with the caption: Is this kidnap victim Annalee Winters? Heir to the Winters pharmaceutical fortune? Ben stared at her frowning features as she'd faced Theresa's mother, and he felt one small consolation. The article hadn't mentioned anything about Dalton Falls...not yet. Tomorrow or the next day a follow-up article would probably appear, if they managed to find more information.

Ben was determined they wouldn't get it from him. Even if he never got the opportunity to see Anna again, he wasn't going to lead the world to her door.

To get away from Dalton Falls and the remaining reporters, Ben drove the two-laned roads of Wayne County, but his mind kept drifting back to Anna, to what he could or couldn't have done differently. If she were just a normal woman, he could rightfully ask her to stay, ask her to wait to see if things could work out between them. But Anna wasn't normal. She was the woman who lived on

top of a mountain with only guard dogs and a shotgun for company. She was the woman whose picture made the front page for doing nothing more
than walking the earth.

Because of the kidnapper.

Ben had had no other response from the FBI
even though he'd called the agent in charge and
left a message that time was definitely of the es-
sence. The wait filled Ben with worry and with
hope. He'd been so convinced he might be able to
help Anna. Then again, he'd thought he could help
Sharon, too. But she'd been caught in the crossfire,
out of his reach, and killed in front of his eyes. He
hadn't even had the chance to say goodbye.

A radio call interrupted Ben's morbid thoughts.

"Deputy Ravenswood, what's your 20?"

Ben glanced around as he picked up the mike.
"I'm approximately three miles east of the 52/19
crossroads."

"Good. Stop by Mr. Hickerson's farm. He
called in about some vandalism."

Ben slowed his cruiser and prepared to make a
U-turn. "I'm on my way."

At least he had something to occupy his mind,
although the prospect didn't really make him feel
better. After Anna left for good he'd have more
time to occupy than he liked to consider. And it
would be spent alone.

THERE WERE FOUR OPEN SUITCASES on the living room floor. Theresa had put Belle in one, cushioned by a fluffy blanket, so she could watch the baby and pack at the same time.

"I know you're on the run, but I don't think the airlines will let you ship the baby in a suitcase," Anna said, smiling down at Belle. For some unfathomable reason, she was determined to keep things upbeat.

"I'd probably try it if we could both fit in there," Theresa said, folding a blouse with the store tags still attached before placing it in the nearest suitcase.

Theresa seemed to be taking her impending departure harder than expected. Anna frowned, then sat down on the rug next to her. "Just think, you're going to a new place, an exciting place," she said, feeling like a New Age tour guide. "The sun, the ocean… California is so different from here, you and Belle are going to love it."

"I'm not worried about California," Theresa said, continuing to fold her new clothes methodically. "I'm just worried that I'll do the wrong thing. That I'll mess everything up."

"You'll be fine," Anna comforted. "You didn't know what to do with Belle at first." She ran a finger lightly over the baby's fine hair. "Now you're a veteran mom."

Theresa looked at Anna then, her eyes showing

her apprehension. "I don't know if I can do it by myself."

"Sure you can," Anna said, knowing firsthand people could accomplish almost anything if they had to. She herself had survived being held captive by a lunatic and stayed alive for over fifteen years by using her brain, and her father's money. Theresa would have to learn the same lessons. Some of them, she already knew. "You ran through the woods for three days pregnant and on your own and eluded every lawman in the county before my dogs caught you. You'll survive and make a new life in California because there's no other choice for you or for Belle." Wishing she had better advice, Anna patted the girl's knee.

"I know you're gonna be fine."

Theresa stopped folding and pulled a tissue out of her pocket to blot her eyes. "The trial sort of set my nerves on edge. It reminded me of all the mistakes I've made so far."

"The trial was the best place to start your new beginning. Each time you get scared, you just remember the meanness in Jimmy's eyes. Then say to yourself, you'll do whatever it takes to never have to look into those eyes again."

IT TOOK OVER AN HOUR and a half for Ben to calm Mr. Hickerson down about his catfish pond. It seemed that some kids on four-wheelers had dumped almost a half a cord of firewood into the pond, probably by driving into the stack repeatedly. It looked like a lot of work in the name of so-called fun.

That was one of the differences between the city and country. City vandals were more likely to use a can of spray paint and not work up a sweat. Country teenagers weren't afraid of a little hard work even if it was against the law.

"I know who they are," Mr. Hickerson insisted.

"Well, I can't arrest them unless you or I catch them at it. But if you'll write down their names, I'll see if a call to the respective parents will help."

Mr. Hickerson snorted disdainfully. "It won't help to call that Taylor boy's daddy. He's worse than the son."

Ben didn't say anything, although he agreed with the farmer's assessment. Sometimes it seemed like meanness ran in families. "Maybe I'll get lucky and catch them riding on the blacktop with those four-wheelers. I could impound the vehicles and teach 'em a lesson."

Mr. Hickerson just shook his head.

It took another twenty minutes before Ben pulled out of the Hickerson driveway. He'd just turned west toward Dalton Falls when his radio crackled to life.

"Ben. Sheriff says to get into town. ASAP."

As always, Ben's mind went to Anna. "What's happening?"

"There's been some kind of mix-up. That Cintero boy has been released."

"What?"

"Sheriff said he'd fill you in."

Ben slammed down the mike and hit the switch for his siren and lights. He'd use them until he hit the city limits, then he'd shut them down. Time to be quiet and careful. He had to get to Annalee.

THE PHONE RANG at a quarter to four. Anna jumped, then felt silly. She was getting worse than Theresa, keyed up over every sound or movement. Surely nothing had gone wrong yet.

"Hello?"

"Anna? It's Ben."

Anna would have been happy to hear his voice if the tone of it hadn't been so tense. "What's wrong?"

"Theresa is there with you, right?"

Confused, Anna said, "Well yes. She's still in Georgia but she's not here right now." After Theresa had made a list of things she needed to take with her like toiletries and a few baby things, she and Anna had decided it was time for her to get used to doing things on her own. So they'd strapped the car seat into the rear of the rental and

Theresa had driven herself and Belle into Dalton Falls.

"She went into town. Now tell me what's going on," Anna demanded. Ben was scaring her. She knew from experience it was better to face reality and take action than to be trapped by fear.

"Jimmy Cintero is out of jail." Ben's voice sounded flat and official. A police officer on duty.

"How can that be? They found him guilty. He was supposed to be sentenced today." Anna fought the rising panic inside. She had just sent Theresa into town...alone.

"There was a mix-up at the jail. He was put with the wrong group of prisoners. His paperwork had been pulled for the trial, so when he called a bail bondsman, they released him early this morning."

"So he's been free for six or eight hours." Plenty of time to get to Dalton Falls. Anna's heart clenched.

"I'll go look for her," Ben said.

"I'm coming, too," she said, and in a rush, hung up the phone.

She pulled back her hair and covered it with a baseball cap. Then she grabbed her keys, picked up her shotgun and headed for her truck. All the way into town she tried to pray. The problem was that she'd forgotten how a long time ago. She knew there were things she ought to be thankful for, but it always seemed the bad things out-

weighed any help she'd received. But she would
pray if it would save Theresa and Belle. *Oh my
God. Belle.*

Anna forced herself to drive slowly along Main
Street, searching for the rental car. At least it was
nondescript. No one could connect it to Theresa or
Anna. She finally spotted it in the public parking
lot at the end of the square. No way to tell which
store Theresa might be in. The most important
thing was to get her out of sight, then get her on
a plane.

Jimmy's back in town.

As she pulled into a parking space near the
rental, she saw two police cruisers turn onto the
square. One of them parked in front of the diner,
the other kept going. She decided to leave the shotgun in the truck for the time being. She needed to
be quick and unobtrusive.

The Baby Place was the most likely destination
for a woman who needed baby things. As she entered the small, wide-open store, Anna could see
for herself Theresa wasn't there. The woman behind the counter, after initially being stunned silent
by having to face the Witch of Rain Mountain,
finally, haltingly explained that, yes, the girl and
her baby had been there but she'd already left. And
no, she didn't know where she'd gone.

As Anna moved on down the row of businesses,
stopping at windows and looking in stores, she

gathered more and more attention. Soon she heard a voice she should have recognized as trouble.

"Annalee?"

As she turned, the man smiled. "You're Annalee Winters, aren't you?"

"That's not my name," she declared, and walked away. But he didn't leave. Soon there were three others following her, asking questions or trying to get her attention.

By the time she reached the drugstore, she was frantic. The growing group of reporters and onlookers behind her made her want to run. But she couldn't run, she had to find Theresa. She also had to find a few moments to get herself together or she'd do something this town would never forget, like start screaming and pulling her hair out in the middle of Main Street. Hoping for an escape, she pushed on the entrance door of the drugstore, but it didn't budge. Her heart pounded faster. She pushed again. It couldn't be closed. When she glanced up to gauge the problem, she met the eyes of Irene, the troublesome cashier.

Her hand was still on the lock.

"Let me in, please," Anna asked, trying not to let her growing hysteria scare the woman.

But the cashier seemed frozen while the vultures, as Anna thought of them, closed around her. Anna closed her eyes and rested the top of her baseball cap against the glass barrier of the door.

Be calm. Think. It had been a very long time since she'd been caught unprepared like this. If she really had been a witch, she would've wished to be ugly and terrifying in the next heartbeat. She took a shaky breath. Without her dogs or her shotgun she had no defense but her silence.

Run away, run away. Hide.

Suddenly, after what seemed like eons, there was a click and the door swung inward. Anna opened her eyes to see the woman who'd refused to wait on her the week before.

"Get in here," she said, but the expression on her face betrayed her distaste.

Anna didn't care. Any port in a storm—friendly or not. She stepped through the door and, when the reporters tried to follow, Irene, dragon that she was, said, "Not you," then shoved the door closed and locked it. That left her and Anna alone together.

"Thank you," Anna said, making an effort to get herself calm enough to think. She was amazed the woman had opened the door to her at all.

Irene seemed to think an explanation for her behavior was required, as though she might be called to account later by her peers. "Well, whatever you are, at least you live in this town. You're one of us. Those people are outsiders." She sniffed and stared through the door, giving them her best amateur evil eye.

By force of habit, Anna sidled out of the reporters' line of sight. She didn't need any more pictures taken of her through the glass. Irene followed but not too closely.

"Was there a young girl with a baby in here this afternoon?" Anna asked, dismissing the reporters and getting to the most important subject—Theresa.

"Why yes. That is the sweetest baby..." A dawning comprehension changed her features. "Is that who you were buying the baby things for the other day? When I..."

"Yes." What difference would it make now if everybody knew. Theresa had to leave immediately, as soon as Anna found her.

There was a tapping on the door, but they both ignored it.

"She was in here, oh, about thirty minutes ago, bought a breast pump and some pacifiers."

"Did everything seem okay? She wasn't nervous or in a hurry?"

"No," the cashier said. "She even let me hold the baby. Funny thing though, she wouldn't tell me the baby's name. Said it was bad luck until she was christened." The woman looked puzzled. "I'd never heard that before, but then these mountain folk have their ways."

If Theresa hadn't been in a hurry, it probably meant she had no idea yet about Jimmy, about the danger. But it also could mean she'd been stalling for time, hoping someone would see her.

"Was she alone?" Anna asked, thinking of the occasions she'd had to stay quiet and follow instructions in order to keep from being hurt.

"Yes, just her and the baby," the cashier answered. "Mrs. Anderson was in here with her grandson and that was it."

A louder tapping sounded on the door, causing Irene to frown. "If you break that glass—" she began in a loud voice then stopped. "Oh, it's Deputy Ben."

Anna moved farther down the aisle as Irene went to let Ben into the store. She desperately wanted to see him, and because of that unfamiliar neediness she wasn't sure what she might do when she did. Bursting into tears and throwing herself into his arms wouldn't help the situation. It would only give people more to talk about, more leverage to hurt her and Ben. And it wouldn't help Theresa. Tears made it hard to see what was right in front of you.

She heard Ben's deep voice obviously addressing the crowd outside. "You people need to disperse or I might have to cite you for loitering, or holding a parade without a permit. I might even work up a charge of stalking if I can get the judge on the phone. So, move along."

Anna heard the door shut. Ben was speaking into

the radio clipped to his shoulder when she finally turned. "Is there anyone free to do some crowd control downtown?" he asked, but his gaze was locked on hers.

"Right now, no," the dispatcher answered. "I'll see who I can find."

Anna could barely breathe and her knees felt like Jell-O, for two reasons. Being chased had brought back her painful past more efficiently than any psychiatrist or hypnotist. Her heart was pounding so hard she felt light-headed.

And then there was Ben. Each time she walked away from him, she carried a vision of his face in her mind, thinking it would be a substitute for the real man. But then, when he appeared before her in flesh and blood, any memory she had seemed to pale and fall to dust.

Love. Hormones or wanting to be normal weren't enough to make her heart ache with joy and sadness at the mere sight of him. She'd fallen in love with Ben Ravenswood. The total surprise of the revelation robbed her of the ability to speak.

Ben, every centimeter the deputy sheriff, stopped just short of running her down and asked, "Are you all right?"

As she nodded yes, she could see the anger and concern in his eyes. It caused her to draw in a shaky breath of relief. Ben was there, he would help.

He glanced over the top of the store displays toward the door, then at Irene. "Which way is the back door?"

"Through the pharmacy. Follow me," she answered, and moved in the designated direction.

Taking Anna's arm, he brought her closer to him. "We need to get you out of here."

Anna allowed Ben to lead her. His touch radiated strength and she felt her limbs respond. She had to pull herself together.

"What about Theresa?" she asked. "We have to find her."

"We've got every available officer looking for her. We'll find her. You need to go home. With these reporters in town, we'll end up pulling people off the search for crowd control."

The sting of that truth caught Anna unprepared. She, because of who she was, couldn't help her only friend. A cold shiver ran through her. And soon, someone besides reporters might show up in town looking for Anna herself.

They reached the back door and Irene prepared to open it but Ben stopped her.

"I saw your truck in the public lot," he said to Anna. "We'll head straight for it. Okay?"

Anna nodded.

Ben opened the door partway and looked outside. He took Anna's arm again.

"Irene, keep the front door locked for another ten minutes or so, all right?"

"You got it."

They moved quickly past the backs of the different stores until they reached the parking lot. Even though Anna had long legs, she almost had to jog to keep up with Ben. As they rounded the corner Anna stopped.

"The car's gone."

Ben tugged her forward, not willing to waste any time.

"I parked next to the rental Theresa was driving and now it's gone." Anna felt tears itching behind her eyelids. If the reporters hadn't cornered her, she would have found Theresa.

"Give me a description of the car," he ordered, and Anna complied.

They reached the truck, Ben unlocked the driver door, handed Anna the keys, then walked around the front of the vehicle and got in on the passenger side. As soon as he slammed the door, he yanked off Anna's baseball cap, tossed it on the dash and pulled her into his arms.

"I don't even have the words," he said close to her ear. "I didn't understand before, but now I do. How in the hell have you faced this alone for fifteen years?"

Anna didn't know how she had either, but she knew one thing: her problems at this point were small compared to Theresa's. She couldn't sit still and allow Ben to give her the comfort only he seemed able to provide. No matter how much she needed it, needed him. She had to help Theresa.

"We've got to find her, Ben." Anna fought the feeling of helplessness. "We've got to." Then she stared into Ben's determined gaze.

"I will, I swear. But first we've got to get you out of here."

"But—"

"No buts. I want you to drive out of town on Mitchellville Road, watch your rearview mirrors and make a few unexpected turns. Don't go back to Rain Mountain until you're positive you're not being followed. Will you do that?" Before she could reply, he went on, "And remember, there's a good chance Jimmy Cintero hightailed it out of state."

Anna couldn't depend on chance. "I was going to check the post office. We had some packages to pick up."

"I'll check the post office. You go home."

Not listening to anything but her own fears for Theresa, Anna had a sudden inspiration. "I know, I'll go to Juney's. Maybe she went there."

"That's a good idea." Ben ran his hands along her upper arms. "Just please, be safe. I can't concentrate on Theresa when I'm worrying about you. I'll be in touch and I'll come up to the cabin as soon as I can." He kissed her mouth, one soft kiss, interrupting her fearful thoughts and leaving her breathless. "You know you have my heart," he said gently. "No matter what you do, or where you go, part of me goes with you."

Before Anna could untangle all the words she wanted to say, he settled her cap back on her head, opened the door, locked it and got out. Gripping the steering wheel with tears distorting her vision, she watched his broad back as he walked away.

BEN TOOK HIS TIME heading back to his patrol car, although every muscle in his body wanted to hurry. He purposely avoided going anywhere near the drugstore and didn't use his portable radio to give the description of the rental car. Not only did he have to worry about Jimmy Cintero, there were also those damn reporters. If someone overheard him, he might see the description of Theresa and the car on the front page in the morning.

Or worse.

He arrived at his patrol car ten minutes later and casually glanced toward the parking lot where he'd left Anna. Her truck was gone and he could see that most of the people following her earlier were still camped out in front of the drugstore. He allowed himself one small feeling of accomplishment. At least she got out of town.

He didn't waste any more time. "Be advised.

Subject, Theresa Smith driving a white 1999 Buick Century, Fulton County tag—no number available."

"Ten-four. Buick Century, white, Fulton County plates." Then after a pause. "Deputy Ravenswood, Sheriff wants you in the station ASAP."

Ben's heart seemed to freeze in his chest. That meant he didn't want to put what he had to say out on the radio. It wouldn't do any good to ask why, but a feeling of impatience and dread settled over him. "I'm on my way."

First, as he promised, he drove by the post office and found no sign Theresa had been there—the packages remained unclaimed. By the time he got to the station, several bad scenarios had played through his mind. If Theresa had disappeared or they'd already found her car empty, he didn't want to think how Anna would take the news. It dawned on him that since her arrival in Wayne County, the police had spent more time searching for Theresa than any other person in his memory. Yet he hoped he wasn't about to hear news to end the search for good.

He left his cruiser in a red zone and hurried through the back door of the station. A few strides later he stuck his head through the open doorway of the sheriff's office.

"You want to see me?"

The sheriff shuffled some of the papers in front

of him, not giving any indication of bad news, or good. "Close the door," he said. "Sit down."

Ben couldn't wait. "Have they found her?" he asked as he shut the door.

After a slight hesitation, the sheriff answered, "Oh, the girl. No, not yet. I called you in about this." He handed Ben several faxed sheets. "The FBI came up with a match for the DNA."

Skimming the sheet of lab results, Ben flipped the pages until he was staring at the mug shot of a man in his late thirties or early forties—black, unkempt hair, a couple of days' worth of beard. He had what Ben would describe as a wiry build, not muscular but strong just the same. It was the cold expression in the man's eyes that gave Ben a shock. Even a police officer who dealt with criminals on a regular basis wasn't immune to the sight of a stone-cold predator. Was this the man who'd hurt Annalee? The possibility made him feel queasy, then furious. He flipped to the last page where there was a second photo, a close-up of the man's bare chest and arms. His chest was covered by several prison tattoos—Christ on the cross with the words Jesus Saves below it. Nothing unique or well-done. On each arm, however, there was an elaborate tattoo of a tiger's face, worked in such fine detail they seemed alive, watching the world from their cage inside the flesh. Only, instead of gold and black, these tigers were red...like blood.

A rush of adrenaline sizzled through Ben's nerves. He would dedicate his life to finding this sick pervert and making sure he never hurt any young girls again. For Anna's sake, for his own peace of mind. No wonder Anna had gone to such lengths to get lost in the world, if this was what had been hunting for her. "Do they have any leads on his whereabouts?"

"Better than that."

Ben dragged his attention away from the menacing tigers and looked up at the sheriff. "What's better than that?"

"Read the report. He died in prison eight years ago—stabbed twenty-eight times by another inmate. Jailhouse justice. If he's your man, he's already dancin' with the devil."

THERESA HADN'T GONE to Juney's. Juney herself wasn't home when Anna stopped, but her daughters had been there most of the afternoon. No Theresa.

The small feeling of success Anna had clung to after seeing Ben and getting out of town without notice faded. Her many fears seemed to be closing in again as she turned onto the road that led up Rain Mountain. She did her best to think positively, to be ready to find Theresa at the cabin waiting impatiently for her to come home. But she was better at being prepared than being positive. She glanced down at the shotgun, then back up to the road in front of her.

Where are you, Theresa?

TRANSCRIPTION of taped session with female X, 16 years old. Excerpted from psychiatric evaluation of Dr. Antony Desillio, Ph.D., State of New York.

"Tell me about your mother."

"I barely knew her."

"Your father lent me a photograph of her. Would you like to see it?"

(Patient nods)

"She's beautiful."

"That's you in her lap. Do you have any memories from that time?"

(Patient shakes head)

"Would you like to be someone's mother someday?"

(Patient returns photo)

"No."

"Why is that?"

"I don't know how."

CHAPTER FIFTEEN

FIFTEEN MINUTES LATER, Anna drove down her own driveway and found Theresa sitting on the front porch in a rocker with Belle in her arms. It should have made Anna smile. Laugh even. She'd been running all over town searching for Theresa and she'd come home. But if life could be drawn in simple lines like a cartoon, then the question below it might read, "What is wrong with this picture?" Only two things were out of place: the rental car and the smirking man sitting in the rocker next to Theresa, holding a lethal-looking knife.

Very aware of the loaded shotgun at her feet, Anna parked the truck in her usual spot and shut down the engine. Her fear had disappeared. She'd always found it easier dealing with what was in front of her rather than worrying about what she couldn't see. She lowered the window, stalling for time. Whatever happened, she wasn't going to make this easy for Jimmy Cintero.

"Don't even think of driving away," Jimmy said. He held up the knife in a twisting motion.

"Unless you don't care how much I cut this bitch of mine."

Anna had no intention of leaving. He'd invaded her sanctuary, threatened her friend. No, Annalee wasn't leaving. "What do you want?"

"Let's see." He lightly touched the tip of the knife to his chin. "I want money and whatever else I see I need. I'll take that rental car, and of course—" he pulled Theresa close in a parody of a hug "—my girl and her kid."

Her kid.

He'd gotten the important part right, anyway. Belle was not part of him even if he had fathered her. He didn't deserve her.

Anna opened the truck door and got out, leaving the gun behind. She'd rather face a knife than her own shotgun. She had some knowledge of knives—she'd felt the sting and survived. As she walked forward, Jimmy lost the flavor of his relaxed, I'm-in-charge-here mood. He stood, dragging Theresa up with him.

"I want you to cook me something to eat, too. I didn't get no breakfast in jail this morning. They were too busy letting me go." He smiled mockingly.

"Why didn't you invite him in?" Anna asked Theresa.

Obviously too afraid to speak, Theresa just

stared at Anna with bone-deep terror showing on her face, and shook her head.

"I saw them dogs in there," Jimmy said. "You better lock 'em up or I'll cut 'em up." He made a slashing gesture with the knife.

Slowly stepping up onto the porch, Anna said, "Okay, I'll go in first and lock them up."

"Don't think about using the phone—" Theresa made a heartrending sound of protest as Jimmy pulled the baby out of her arms. "Or I'll end what never shoulda been started."

Gazing into his hard, angry eyes caused something inside Anna to take flight, soaring high off the rocky cliff of sanity into the darkness. The years of hiding and being afraid hadn't helped—violence had still found her.

It was then she decided to kill Jimmy Cintero. One way or another, if he hurt Belle, he was not leaving this place.

No more run away, run away, hide.

"I'll lock up the dogs," she said. "No problem." Unbelievably, her voice sounded calm, normal, even though every nerve ending in her body felt coiled and ready to fight. She thought of the shotgun in the truck and began to work out a plan to retrieve it.

Jimmy smiled. "You do that. You lock 'em up, then start cooking." He gave Theresa a little

shove. "This bitch never could cook worth
a damn."

AN HOUR LATER, technically off duty, Ben checked
with dispatch one more time to see if anything new
had come in on Theresa Smith or the fugitive
Jimmy Cintero.

Nothing.

He'd been chafing at the bit to drive out to Rain
Mountain. And now that he'd done everything he
could do in Theresa's case, he picked up the phone
and dialed Anna's cabin. He thought with Theresa's boyfriend on the loose, it might be better to
give her some notice he'd be there soon. She'd be
twice as nervous as usual. He wasn't looking forward to telling her about the lack of progress in
the search.

As he listened to the phone ring, he felt at least
some satisfaction about the long day. Although he
wouldn't have the opportunity of hunting the man
down himself, he had the information and proof to
finally put Anna's very real fears to rest. If he
could do that, then he might have the time to per-
suade her to stay on Rain Mountain. To convince
her that he needed her, that they needed each other.
He would keep her safe.

The phone continued to ring and Ben's high-
flown hopes began to crumble. Where was she? It
would be dark in another hour. Was she walking

the fence line with the dogs? By the tenth ring his hard-earned knowledge of Anna produced a terrible thought. She wouldn't be out with the dogs when Theresa was missing. She'd be out looking for the girl.

Damn. He hung up the phone. He felt like kicking himself for believing she'd actually do what she'd promised. He knew how independent and stubborn Anna could be. And how protective she was of the girl. After a day of searching, now he'd have to find Anna.

On the way out of the station, he issued a lookout on her truck and asked to be notified if anyone saw her. Then he got in his four-by-four and drove to Juney Bridger's. It was the last place she'd mentioned going. If he'd believed in luck, he could hope he'd find the three of them there, Juney, Theresa and Annalee having some kind of female conspiracy conversation. But luck hadn't been his best friend in the past.

He passed one Wayne County patrol car on the drive to Rain Mountain. He flashed his lights and slowed, stopping driver-window to driver-window. It was Rudy.

"Haven't seen anything stranger than a possum that actually made it across the road without gettin' hit," Rudy said. "You suppose that girl is off in the woods again?"

"No. Not this time. She's in that rental car but

where the car is, is another question,'' Ben answered. ''I'm headed up to Rain Mountain, let me know if you see Annalee in her truck.''

''You'll be the first,'' Rudy said. ''Should I stop her?''

Ben thought of the shotgun in the truck and decided not to pit Rudy against Annalee. For one thing, after the day she'd been through, she might take any interference as a threat. And, for another, Rudy would lose.

''Nah. Just let me know when and where.''

With a nod and a wave Rudy pulled away.

JUNEY BRIDGER WAS STANDING on her porch when Ben drove into the driveway. She walked over to meet him as he was getting out of his truck. He could tell by the concerned look on her face that Theresa and Annalee weren't there.

''Have you seen them?'' he asked.

She shook her head no, hugged herself and slowly rubbed her arms even though the weather was mild. ''Annalee was here earlier. Sarah spoke to her. Haven't seen either one since.''

''Do you know where they are?''

Ben wasn't exactly sure why he asked the question, but when he did, Juney's expression changed. As though it pained her to answer.

''Not exactly. But I know one thing. Tonight will change lives.'' Juney extended a hand and rested it on his forearm. Her skin was so warm it made him jump, but she held the contact. "Annalee thinks she can save Theresa by sacrificing herself. She doesn't know about the baby."

With Juney's prophetic words ringing in his ears, Ben had the sudden image of Annalee holding her shotgun. Firing. Not once but twice, then three times.

"What about Theresa's baby?" Ben asked, filled with dread.

"Not Theresa's. The baby you made with Annalee." Juney removed her hand. "You need to find her, right now."

BELLE HAD BEGUN TO CRY when the repeated ringing of the unanswered phone woke her up. As Theresa did her best to quiet the baby, all of them sat tensely until the phone stopped.

Ben.

It had to be Ben calling. Instead of relief, Anna had felt pure terror. She had to do something before Ben showed up. At least she knew what she was facing. It would take every trick she knew to protect Theresa and Belle. Ben would walk into the situation without any warning of the danger and could be hurt. She pushed the image of Ben in pain away. No, she wouldn't allow that to happen as long as she had breath in her body.

Better her than Ben.

Ben couldn't help them now. Besides, he couldn't be a part of what she had to do. He'd try to stop her. She had to do it on her own.

At Jimmy's insistence, she'd prepared an abbreviated dinner of warmed-up, leftover fried chicken, potato salad and sliced tomatoes. Jimmy had insisted on cutting the tomatoes himself and ordered the two women to sit down and eat so he could keep an eye on everyone. Anna had filled Theresa's plate, after Jimmy had taken what he wanted, then fixed one for herself, but she couldn't have swallowed a sip of water much less solid food.

Theresa sat, completely silent, ignoring the food and holding Belle as though any moment the baby would be snatched away from her. Anna wanted to comfort her but refrained. Theresa would have to hold herself together a little while longer so Anna could concentrate on Jimmy.

The baby continued to cry.

"I have to change her diaper," Theresa said in a low, halting voice. She kept her gaze down, on her plate, on the baby, anywhere but on the man who sat next to her.

Jimmy bit into another chicken leg as if he intended to ignore her words. But then he tossed the chicken down onto the plate in disgust and turned to her.

"Well, don't just sit there. Do it. How can I eat with that noise?"

Theresa's chair made a scraping sound on the floor as she pushed away from the table.

"Wait a minute."

She stopped, looking afraid to breathe.

He picked up the knife he'd threatened her with earlier, wiped it clean with the edge of the tablecloth and held it up for her to see.

Anna watched the blade flash with the reflection of the light, silver, like moonlight, and she knew it was speaking to her. Telling her it was time.

"Don't do anything stupid," he said to Theresa.

She nodded.

He made a show of putting the knife next to his plate and patting it in place. Then he picked up his fork to continue his meal while Theresa took slow careful steps toward the bedroom she and Belle shared.

Anna moved her hands to the edge of the table and tightened her grip. Her own bedroom door was eight feet away. Behind that door were her best weapons, Diva and Hunter.

Jimmy pointed to her plate with his fork. "I told you to eat. Now eat!"

Anna propelled herself upward, taking the heavy table with her. With all her strength she shoved the weight of it on top of him. Dishes crashed and Jimmy yelped, falling backward as the table hit his knees then pushed him to the floor. In seconds, Anna had made it to the bedroom door.

Hunter was first out of the bedroom. "Get him!" she ordered. "Attack!"

There was no uncertainty on his part. The big dog leaped at the intruder, and a moment later Jimmy let out a screech of pain. Unable to find his knife fast enough in the debris from the table, Jimmy howled and cursed as he tried to kick the dogs away. Hunter went for one arm while Diva sank her teeth into his leg.

Theresa watched trancelike from the hallway, clutching Belle but making no move to help Jimmy.

Jimmy, bleeding and obviously furious, fought loose and made it to the back door. He got it open and wedged it between him and the dogs long enough to get outside.

"I'll kill you!" He screamed. "I'll kill all of you!"

Anna didn't waste any time. She yanked the door open and sent the dogs out on his heels. "Get him!" she ordered again. Then with the barking and snarling dogs keeping Jimmy busy, she ran through the cabin and out the front door.

She returned with the shotgun and a box of shells in her hands.

Theresa was still standing where Anna had left her, obviously in shock. As Anna stuffed some of the shells from the box in her pockets, she asked, "Do you have the keys to the rental?"

Theresa nodded.

Anna crossed the room and grabbed her by the arm, using one hand to shake her until Belle whimpered and Theresa seemed more coherent. "Get in the car and go. Like we planned. Do you understand me?"

The dogs were farther away now, chasing Jimmy to who knows where, and Anna knew she couldn't waste any more time if she was going to end this. Here and now.

She gripped Theresa's upper arm until the girl flinched. "Put Belle in that car and leave!"

Some of the color returned to Theresa's features. She nodded and pulled the keys out of her pocket. Then she seemed to grasp the realization Anna was staying behind.

"What are you going to do?"

"I'm going to make sure he doesn't come after you."

Theresa's eyes looked haunted for a moment. She threw an arm around Anna and hugged her, hard. "I'm so s-sorry."

"Get out of here. You know what to do," Anna said, before the emotion of losing her only friend could soften her heart. She needed the coldness of a killer, the focused menace of the bad man, for what she was about to do. She stepped away, grabbed a flashlight and headed out the back door, following her dogs, following Jimmy Cintero.

ANNA WALKED AWAY from Theresa without looking back. She couldn't. Any feelings she experienced would sap her strength, take away the advantage. She had to go inside, to the place where nothing and no one could touch her. She couldn't afford to feel right now.

About thirty feet from the back of the house, she stopped to listen. Jimmy had run up the hill instead of down the driveway. Not very smart. It was harder to run uphill with something faster chasing you. In this case she supposed he really didn't have a lot of choice. He didn't know the area, or have any idea what he was up against. A full-grown man might fight off one dog the size of Diva. Add a big male like Hunter, and any advantage disappeared.

Grimly she started up the hill after them. The sound of breaking brush and snapping tree branches had stopped. Now it was just the barking and snarling of the dogs. They wouldn't kill him, but they could make him wish he was dead. He'd probably climbed a tree or found a corner to hide in. Didn't matter, he wasn't getting away.

Headlights flashed behind her. Anna glanced back briefly and watched Theresa maneuver the rental car down the driveway a little faster than necessary. She smiled in grim satisfaction. After tonight Theresa would be safe. It was the one true gift she could give her friend and her godchild. A life different from her own.

BEN TOOK THE CORNER at the bottom of Rain Mountain a little too fast, causing his truck to fishtail in the gravel. He steered into the skid but didn't slow down. After his visit to Juney, every instinct he'd ever claimed told him that Anna was on her land, holed up. In trouble. The fact that she hadn't answered the phone only meant he might be too late.

He knew it couldn't be the man who'd haunted her. He was dead, although Anna didn't know that. There were a thousand possibilities, but the most likely one seemed to be Theresa and Cintero. He could deal with that one, if he could just get there.

Darkness tended to come quickly in the mountains, and already the first star had appeared in the twilight of the northern sky. The lack of light might be a blessing or a curse. Good for hiding, useless for searching. Ben wasn't sure which he'd be doing soon.

Halfway up the mountain, the flash of headlights farther uphill startled him. The only traffic on this road would be coming from Anna's. He switched on his own lights and braced himself just as a white car came careening around the curve heading straight for him. They barely missed colliding and the effort to stop sent a storm of gravel and dust into the air. Before the dust had settled, Ben was out of his truck with a flashlight and jogging to the car.

"Are you all right?" he asked Theresa as he illuminated the inside of the rental car. He saw the baby, still securely held by the baby seat in the back.

She nodded, her hands gripping the steering wheel. Then, as though she'd received an electric shock, she jumped. She unfastened her seat belt, pushed up to her knees and leaned over the seat to check her daughter.

"She's okay," she said, her voice sounding choked as she settled back behind the steering wheel.

"Where's Anna?"

Theresa looked at him then, and the pain in her features made his heart pound. "Where is she?" He would get an answer if he had to shake it out of her.

"It's too late," she said. Her eyes were already red and puffy, but a new batch of tears made their way down her cheeks.

Ben didn't have time for tears. Before he made any conscious decision, his hand was on the door handle and he'd yanked it open. He stooped down to face her eye-to-eye. "What are you saying? What's happened?"

She simply stared at him then shook her head.

His hand gripped her arm. "Tell me, Theresa. Right now! Have you seen Cintero?"

At the mention of his name, she flinched but remained silent.

Ben straightened and spoke into his portable radio unit. "Deputy Ravenswood requesting backup on Rain Mountain, Annalee Evans's place. Subject Theresa Smith found, fugitive Cintero has been spotted in the area. Rudy, you take charge of the girl, I'm going after Annalee."

He didn't spare Theresa another look. If she wasn't helping and she wasn't in danger then he didn't have any time to waste on her. "Stay here," he said. "A deputy will be here shortly."

As he raced to his truck, she called out to him. "She's going to kill him."

Ben remembered the image he'd had at Juney Bridger's—Anna firing her shotgun. "Not if I can help it," he shouted back as he started his engine and spun gravel once more going uphill.

ANNA MOVED CAREFULLY as she neared the place where the dogs had run Cintero to ground. She listened then squinted through the growing gloom not wanting to be surprised by him. If he got too close, he could overpower her and then she had no doubt her troubles and her life would be over.

Worse, he'd be free to hunt Theresa and Belle. She didn't intend to allow him any more chances.

She heard some thrashing and a curse before the dogs growled and barked in response. She knew he was in front of her, she could see Hunter, but not Cintero. Finally, as close as she was willing to get, she switched on her flashlight.

Cintero had fallen into one of her traps. The irony was so perfect, Anna smiled. She didn't call off the dogs, however.

Cintero started at the light, putting a hand up to ease his eyes. He was up to his armpits, scratched and bloody, and quite a bit worse for wear. "Hey," he called. "I need some help." Then his eyes must have adjusted because he realized who he was addressing.

"You bitch! I think I broke my leg."

The dogs, taking offense at his tone of voice, moved closer, threatening his head and face. Cintero forgot about blocking the light and covered his head instead. "Get these dogs off me!"

He sounded furious and near hysteria. To Anna, that seemed fitting for a man who liked to terrorize women. She therefore allowed the dogs to use their own good judgment. When he stopped thrashing and shouting, they backed off slightly.

"I'm tellin' you, you are gonna pay for this," he threatened, although he didn't raise his voice.

His threats only settled Anna further into her

chosen course of action. She did wonder, distantly, why he wasn't worried by the fact she held him at gunpoint. But his IQ wasn't her concern. Whatever the number, he wouldn't need it where he was headed.

Irony seemed to be the secret word of the day. Jimmy Cintero was going to meet his maker by her hand, and Anna would take his place in the prison system. The irony came into the equation, because Anna had realized prison was probably the only safe place for her. The bad man couldn't find her there. She wouldn't have to use her life to plan her next escape or worry who would recognize her. No decisions, no fears—an attractive proposition. She could read her books, do her time and, for once in fifteen years, feel totally safe.

She'd miss her dogs, though, her beautiful, loyal friends.

And she would miss Ben.

His image rose from her heart to her mind and rattled her composure. He wouldn't understand why she had to do this and she didn't have the words to explain. Theresa's safety, her own peace of mind. But she couldn't think about Ben. Her love for Ben was one of the few gifts life had given her, and the beauty of that gift had no place inside her now. Because things were about to get ugly.

Settled and determined, Anna raised the shotgun before calling the dogs to her side.

BEN HAD REACHED the open front door of the cabin when he heard the distinctive sound of a shotgun blast. He didn't pause to think. He ran straight through the cabin, out the back door and headlong toward the sound.

Anna.

As he ran, Ben heard a man's voice, yelling for help. Still alive. Ben put his head down and ran faster. In a few minutes, which seemed like hours to him, he saw the beam of a flashlight, and he scrambled through the trees toward it. He slowed outside the circle of light. He could see Cintero on the ground, in one of Anna's traps, but he couldn't see Anna clearly.

He took a chance. "Anna, don't do it," he called, the rushing sound of his breath making him unsure of how far his voice would carry. "Anna, it's Ben."

Cintero heard him. "Help! Help me, man. This crazy woman is gonna kill me!"

Anna didn't answer either of them—a bad sign. Ben slowly made his way forward and finally stepped through the trees into the clearing.

"Anna—"

"This bitch is crazy, man—"

Anna fired a second time, causing Ben to flinch. A patch of earth near Cintero rose and disintegrated into a thousand pieces. The silence afterward was so thick Ben could only hear the ringing in his own ears.

"He has to die," Anna said, her voice a distant, unfamiliar sound.

A feeling of doom settled over Ben. He was too far from her to take the gun out of her hands. He only had words—which so far in the dealings between him and Anna had proved to be totally insufficient.

"Don't do it, Anna," he said, knowing it wasn't enough. "Theresa is safe, you're safe. I'm here now and I can handle him."

The gun and the light remained steady, both aimed at Cintero. "He doesn't deserve to be handled. He needs to go away and never come back."

Ben wished he could see her eyes. She sounded as if she was working herself up to killing him, making a case for the death penalty. "I don't want you to go to prison for killing someone as worthless as he is," Ben said, agreeing but disagreeing.

"Hey, she—" Cintero began.

He was interrupted by the pump action of the shotgun, another deadly round being loaded into the chamber.

Ben had run out of choices. He stepped between Anna's gun and the man she seemed determined to kill.

"I want to go to prison," she said, keeping the

gun chest high. "It's the best place for me. Get out of the way."

"The bad man is dead, Anna." Ben held his breath as the gun barrel dipped slightly then rose again. Those words had touched her.

"I don't believe you," she said.

Ben searched for a way to convince her, some indisputable proof. He knew what had stuck in his mind. "Remember when you said you trusted me? I swear to you, it's true. I saw the tigers."

A long silence followed.

"It doesn't matter," she said finally. "I promised Theresa I'd keep her and Belle safe. I can't guarantee that unless I end it here and now."

Ben didn't bother with the argument that the police would keep Cintero in jail. They'd already failed to do so once.

"Don't do it for me then," he said. "I'll make it my mission in life to keep track of him. If he sneezes I'll know who wiped his nose."

More silence.

"You know I'll keep my word." As he waited for a reaction or reply, Ben knew time was running out. If she truly wanted to shoot Jimmy Cintero there was little he could do to stop her, short of shooting her first. So he played the final card he held. The one closest to his heart.

"Juney says we've made a baby."

Silence.

Jimmy Cintero was the furthest thing from his mind in those seconds. His own future was on the line along with those words. "Did you hear me, Anna? Juney says you've got my baby inside you. I don't want him or her to be born in prison. Not for the likes of Cintero. Not even for Theresa."

Ben waited. He heard movement in the trees downhill and figured his backup had arrived.

"If you love me, get out of the way, Ben. Let me have just one clean shot."

"I trust you, and I love you, Anna," Ben said. He knew that ultimately her life and future were in her own hands. No matter how much he wanted to save her, he couldn't. And he couldn't make the decision for her. With his heart pounding in his throat, he stepped aside.

The shotgun blast sounded louder this time because Ben was closer to the gun. And this time, instead of silence, he heard the deputies hurrying through the underbrush and the dogs barking. In three long strides he'd taken the gun from Anna's hands and pulled her into his arms. He turned to look at Jimmy Cintero as the lights from the approaching deputies illuminated the scene.

"That bitch tried to kill me! Look! I'm bleedin'!" he bellowed to the closest deputy as he pointed to a tiny pellet hole in his sleeve. The dogs had spilled more blood than Anna, but the supposed victim hadn't realized that yet. Then he pointed toward Ben. "And he was gonna let her do it. Get me out of here," he ordered, like any law-abiding citizen with the right to be protected by the law.

Flooded with relief, Ben felt like laughing and shouting at the same time. "I would have thought you'd be a better shot than that," he said, holding Anna tight to his side. His eyes were itching suspiciously. If he hadn't been holding a twelve-gauge shotgun with one hand, and the woman he loved with the other, he might have been able to rub the tears of relief out of them. Instead he pushed his face into Anna's hair as she wrapped her arms around him.

"I was aiming at his ego," she mumbled into Ben's shirt. "You're right, he's not worth losing you or our baby's future."

"So, you believe me?" he asked.

She nodded. "And I believe Juney. She's a witch, you know."

TRANSCRIPTION of taped session with female X, 18 years old. Excerpted from psychiatric evaluation of Dr. Antony Desillio, Ph.D., State of New York.

"I am not crazy."

"Final notes: Patient's progress has reached a plateau conventional therapy does not seem able to affect. She has found some relief from the night terrors and paranoia but the home situation and

notoriety sabotages any further progress. It is my recommendation, therefore, that the patient be removed from her home environment and placed in a more structured facility with in-house treatment.

Without that option, the patient will be required to submit to daily therapy sessions, or be forced to a more rigorous drug regimen.

I feel that these measures are proper and necessary for her to reach any sort of normalcy and will petition the courts to comply with what I am sure would be her father's wishes.''

(Postscript written by nurse)

''Patient, Annalee Winters, reported missing. Authorities do not suspect foul play. Family lawyer reported she left with a suitcase and her mother's cello.''

EPILOGUE

EIGHT AND A HALF MONTHS LATER, Ben unloaded the rocking chair from his truck first. Juney Bridger held the door for him as he entered her house and went straight through to the delivery room. Next, he carried his wife inside and settled her into the chair.

"It'll be good to see Theresa again," Anna said, seemingly more excited by the prospect of seeing her friend than the fact she was in labor.

Ben stooped in front of her before glancing at his watch. "I just hope she makes it in time. She barely caught the red-eye from the coast," he said.

Juney, in the process of handing Anna a cup of her special tea, said, "Don't worry. We've got plenty of time. This baby is in no hurry."

Ben looked at her, but she answered his question before he asked it. "He told me so." She dusted her hands together in a gesture of anticipation. "Yep, we're all gonna have us a fine reunion." She placed one hand on Anna's shoulder. "And a brand-new beginning. Isn't that right, Annalee?"

"Yes, ma'am," Anna said without hesitation.

"I just love this job," Juney said and, laughing, she left them alone.

Ben covered one of Anna's hands with his own. "Are you worried?" He knew he'd been more outwardly concerned for her welfare than she seemed to be. He'd even insisted she see a medical doctor instead of relying solely on Juney. The doctor had promptly announced that everything seemed fine and told him not to fuss. Juney's exact words.

"No, I'm not worried. Because of you—" she ran a hand over her extended belly "—and this baby, I have a future. I'm too busy looking forward to spend time worrying. I want to hold this baby in my arms and raise him with you."

THERESA AND BELLE ARRIVED eight hours later, sleepy eyed but happy to be home. They'd made a good start on their new lives, but Deputy Ben, Annalee and the new baby would always be family. Benjamin Thomas Ravenswood II arrived one hour afterward, kicking and squalling and ready to face the world.

The Witch of Rain Mountain had a son, and a husband, and a brand-new start.

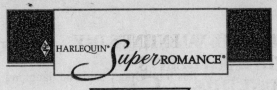

CELEBRATE VALENTINE'S DAY WITH HARLEQUIN®'S LATEST TITLE— Stolen Memories

Available in trade-size format, this collector's edition contains three full-length novels by *New York Times* bestselling authors Jayne Ann Krentz and Tess Gerritsen, along with national bestselling author Stella Cameron.

TEST OF TIME by Jayne Ann Krentz—
He married for the best reason.... She married for the only reason.... Did they stand a chance at making the only reason the real reason to share a lifetime?

THIEF OF HEARTS by Tess Gerritsen—
Their distrust of each other was only as strong as their desire. And Jordan began to fear that Diana was more than just a thief of hearts.

MOONTIDE by Stella Cameron—
For Andrew, Greer's return is a miracle. It had broken his heart to let her go. Now fate has brought them back together. And he won't lose her again...

Make this Valentine's Day one to remember!

Look for this exciting collector's edition on sale January 2001 at your favorite retail outlet.

HARLEQUIN®
Makes any time special™

Visit us at www.eHarlequin.com

PHSM

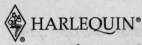

HARLEQUIN®

makes any time special—online...

eHARLEQUIN.com

your romantic life

• Romance 101

♥ Guides to romance, dating and flirting.

• Dr. Romance

♥ Get romance advice and tips from our expert, Dr. Romance.

• Recipes for Romance

♥ How to plan romantic meals for you and your sweetie.

• Daily Love Dose

♥ Tips on how to keep the romance alive every day.

• Tales from the Heart

♥ Discuss romantic dilemmas with other members in our Tales from the Heart message board.

Tyler Brides

It happened one weekend...

Quinn and Molly Spencer are delighted to accept three bookings for their newly opened B&B, Breakfast Inn Bed, located in America's favorite hometown, Tyler, Wisconsin.

But Gina Santori is anything but thrilled to discover her best friend has tricked her into sharing a room with the man who broke her heart eight years ago....

And Delia Mayhew can hardly believe that she's gotten herself locked in the Breakfast Inn Bed basement with the sexiest man in America.

Then there's Rebecca Salter. She's turned up at the Inn in her wedding gown. Minus her groom.

Come home to Tyler for three delightful novellas by three of your favorite authors: Kristine Rolofson, Heather MacAllister and Jacqueline Diamond.

HARLEQUIN®
Makes any time special ™